THE QUEEN'S KNIGHTS
A REBEL LUST TABOO NOVEL

OPHELIA BELL

ANIMUS PRESS

All rights reserved. No part of this book may be reproduced in any form or by any electronic means, including information storage and retrieval systems, without permission in writing from the author, except by a reviewer who may quote brief passages in review.

This is a work of fiction. Names, places, characters, and events are fictitious in every regard. Any similarities to actual events and persons, living or dead, is purely coincidental. Any trademarks, service marks, product names, or named features are assumed to be the property of their respective owners, and are used only for reference. There is no implied endorsement if any of these terms are used.

The Queen's Knights

Copyright © 2022 by Ophelia Bell

Cover Art Designed by Opulent Swag and Designs

Photograph Copyrights © DepositPhotos

Published by Ophelia Bell
UNITED STATES

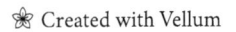

❦ Created with Vellum

CONTENT WARNING

This book includes themes of sexual assault and is about a heroine who prevails over both her attacker and her feelings of helplessness after her assault. Discretion is advised.
- Ophelia Bell

CHAPTER ONE

GWEN

When I offer an invitation to dine, half a dozen men and a couple women raise their hands from the crowd beyond the window. Each one sports a matching light blue ribbon on their left upper arm. Left means they're givers, and they know I'm here to take. Nearly all wear the same ribbon on their opposite arm too. I ignore the other "takers," seeking one whose right arm is unadorned.

A well-built man catches my eye, an inviting smile spreading beneath his jeweled black mask. Without a word, I tilt my chin and Percy nods, stepping toward the door to my playroom, opening it, and pointing.

"You," he says to the man with one blue ribbon.

The man looks flummoxed at first, then his eyes brighten. He glances again at where I rest on my throne and licks his lips before following Percy through the door. The rest of the crowd remains outside the viewing window, some disappointed stares looking back. A couple men leave, not content to merely watch. There are more interactive pursuits to be found in other areas of the club. Most choose to stay for the show.

My chosen subject steps into the center of the room opposite my dais and clears his throat. His Adam's apple bobs with his swallow and he smiles awkwardly. "Ah, I didn't expect to be called on. I'm not sure I know how this works."

He makes it sound as if I called on him to come to the front of class for a presentation. I frown, but don't answer. His voice is vaguely familiar, but I can't place it. His words bring to mind my other life, the one I retreat to Whitewood Club in order to escape. Here I can be queen for a night, fully in control of my own body, my own pleasure, and the partners I choose. No one can touch me without my consent.

Percy steps in, my loyal knight, his muscular bulk blocking my view of my subject for a moment.

"Undress completely," he instructs, "except for your mask. If she still deems you worthy, you'll take your position beneath the throne. What's expected of you should be self-explanatory after that."

The man nods and combs his fingers through his hair. He's handsome, from what I can see. His hair is thick and wavy and inky-black. His eyes are dark behind his mask, but I can't tell whether they're blue or brown. He's as tall as Percy, but leaner, just shy of wiry—though when he strips off his shirt, I reassess, taking in his light brown skin and tattooed biceps, the faint dusting of dark hair that accents a moderate six-pack, and a swimmer's frame, still slightly soft with youth. When he bends over to untie his shoes, the muscles of his tattooed shoulders ripple. The ink appears to go farther than I can see and piques my interest. He's young, but adventurous. Not faint of heart, but willing to submit.

Percy catches my eye, and I give a slight nod to his unspoken question. He's the perfect assistant, his instincts on point when it comes to anticipating my needs, and when my subject sheds his jeans and stands upright again, Percy makes a circular motion in the air.

"Turn slowly so the queen may inspect you."

The man smirks and lifts one shoulder, but obeys. He rotates almost comically slowly, pausing when his back faces me as if he knows I want a good look at his tattoos. The artwork is a striking scene of a knight on horseback slaying a dragon. The man shoots me a glance over one shoulder, then looks at Percy.

"Does she ever give her own commands? Not that I mind a proxy, this is just my first time here, so is this how it always goes, or…?"

"Save your tongue for the real task," Percy says, his tone tinged with humor. "You're going to need it. But every dominatrix makes her own rules—within the bounds of the club's rules, of course."

The man lets out a low laugh, the sound relaxed and confident despite the taut anticipation strung through all his limbs. He swallows again as he turns to face me, his gaze traveling over me in an easy manner, more curious and appreciative than lascivious. His cock thickens slightly when his focus returns to my face.

My face, of all things, half-covered with a mask similar to his own, is what makes him rouse fully—and not even my mouth, the part exposed, but my eyes. We stare at each other, and I force myself to hold his gaze, to avoid dropping it to his crotch to witness his arousal grow. I'm the one in charge here, even though Percy relays the orders. I'm queen on Masquerade Night at Whitewood Club. I sit atop the throne and men line up, hoping to be chosen for a chance to taste my nectar.

This one's smile is hopeful, seeking approval. I maintain

my perfect composure and grant it with a nod.

I haven't been this disarmed by a man in so long, it's both exhilarating and terrifying. But most of all, it gets my blood flowing more than it ever has on Masquerade Night.

The last Saturday of every month is when I get to don this persona, to forget about Gwendolyn Brennan and her weaknesses. I become Queen Justine for a single night, take my place on the throne in room fourteen on the second level of Whitewood Club, and choose who services me.

Because Gwendolyn Brennan didn't get to choose when a violent stranger broke into her university office one evening and forced his cock down her throat, and she's been running from the nightmares ever since.

The images only flash through the back of my mind for a split-second, but I'm already in the zone, behind the veil of the queen. Not only do I hold the power here, but I also have a knight at my side willing to shield me with his body, if it comes to it. Nothing can hurt me, and this masked morsel of youth and vigor is about to submit for the sake of my pleasure.

Percy steps toward me and I lift my feet from the cushioned platform beneath them, spreading my knees wide. My sheer skirt parts at a split down the middle, and as expected, the man's eyes drop to my exposed core. For effect, I shrug the straps of my gown off my shoulders, baring my breasts both to him and our observers beyond the glass. Several members of the audience smile and a few lean closer, ready for the show to begin.

Percy's on his knees, adjusting the moving pieces of the throne for my subject to take his place. The padded footrest rotates and aligns perpendicular to the throne, coming to rest at a slight incline to the floor below my dais. Percy snaps the narrow seat at the end into place. Then he reaches beneath me to lift the headrest up into position.

His face is inches from my pussy, but this part never seems to faze him. He explained at the beginning of my training for this role that he's only here for my comfort and safety, and has never given the impression that he cares about anything else. Having the friendship of a man I can trust so implicitly has been the greatest boon to my healing, but I admit the last couple Masquerade Nights, I've wondered whether he even thinks of me sexually at all.

Finally he unbuckles the wrist straps that attach to either side of the throne and steps to the side, gesturing to the narrow cushioned backrest where my subject must take his place.

"She prefers your wrists restrained. If this is an issue, say so now."

The man blinks, but nods. "Mouth and tongue only. Got it."

Percy leans in to indicate a pair of polished wooden handles above the cuffs on either side of the bench. "These are for leverage, if you need. Do you have any questions? If not, make yourself comfortable."

My plaything is fully erect now. He takes a deep breath and licks his lips, drifting his gaze over the entire tableau once before shaking his head and stepping toward me. He turns and straddles his seat, crouching to lower himself and then lying back. His body is still tightly wound, but he controls his movements like an athlete, hyperaware of his surroundings.

My heartbeat accelerates when he lowers his head between my knees and peers up at me from behind a black velvet mask studded with tiny, glittering onyx gems. His hands brush the backs of my calves when he extends both arms and allows Percy to restrain him.

We stare at each other through my parted thighs, his gaze briefly flicking up to my exposed pussy barely a foot above his head. His lips quirk into a playful smile and he shakes his head. "Please tell me this isn't as close as I'm allowed to get. My tongue isn't that long."

Percy finishes buckling the left cuff around the man's wrist and taps the underside of the backrest. "You're on rails. Just push up with your legs until you're positioned where you like and it'll lock in place. You're good to go. *Bon appétit!*"

With that, Percy steps out of the way into the shadows just behind my throne and whispers into my ear, "I'm here for you, my queen. Just say the word if you need me."

CHAPTER TWO

GWEN

I tilt my head to the side, acknowledging Percy's promise, then look down at my submissive pet for the evening, giving him a somber nod that he may begin. He licks his lips again, and his thighs flex as he pushes against the floor with his feet. His backrest slides up, the motion causing his stiff erection to bounce slightly when it locks into place, his face squarely beneath my spread cheeks. I suppress a gasp of surprise at the sensation of his warm breath gusting against my pussy.

This is the feeling I've ached for since I began this quest to reclaim my power—the anticipation of pleasure strong enough to get my blood pumping even before any contact. I've sought it for six months without success. That isn't to say I haven't enjoyed every evening spent on this throne with a submissive's tongue buried between my thighs, but this is the first time I've craved the pleasure without even being touched.

I force myself into some semblance of composure befitting a queen, force my gaze up from my subject's impressive cock, and scan the onlookers beyond the window. The audience is enthralled, even more so than usual. It seems my submissive is as fascinating to them as he is to me.

"Fucking heaven," he murmurs, and I bite the inside of my mouth to control my reaction to the warmth of his words teasing my sensitive flesh. A deep groan emanates from his chest and his restraints creak. He grips the handholds and his biceps flex as he lifts himself closer to my exposed core, and a moment later, his hot tongue makes one long, languid swipe from my clit all the way to my ass.

I arch my back with a gasp, so surprised by the immensity of the pleasure I nearly lose track of my surroundings. I reach up to grip the carved finials at the top corners of my throne and spread my legs wider.

Behind me, Percy lets out a breath of surprise as if he's just as invested in my pleasure as I am. I tilt my head back to look at him. Our gazes lock past our masks, and for the first time since I've known him, I catch a spark of true desire in his eyes. I've never offered an invitation for him to join in before, and he's never expressed an interest. But tonight I throw caution to the wind.

"You have my permission to touch me, Percival," I whisper.

His lips part and he dry-swallows, then blinks as if he's coming out of a trance.

"Gwen… er… my queen, it would be my absolute honor to assist in giving you pleasure. May I?"

A thick lock of blond hair falls over his forehead as he looks down at me, first at my mouth before his gaze drifts to my breasts. I release the top of the throne and drop my hands to the arms, pushing my breasts up in invitation. My attention splits between the expert tongue buried in my pussy, lapping at my clit, and the lightest brush of Percy's fingertips against my skin as he reaches over my shoulders to cup my breasts.

My throne has a low, contoured back that swoops up on either side to tall, carved posts. It's wide enough for Percy to dip his head and brush his mouth down the column of my throat as he begins to tease my nipples. I let my head fall back against his shoulder and give into the urge to moan. My audience stares wide-eyed as I involuntarily rock my hips on my seat, wishing for closer contact with that devious tongue beneath me. I let my eyelids fall shut, picturing the wicked smile the man gave me just before his face disappeared from view, as if he knew exactly how hypnotic his tongue could be.

For the first time since taking the role of Queen Justine, I'm utterly at my subject's mercy rather than the other way around. Even though he's shackled to the chair, I'm powerless to control a thing.

He must sense my need for deeper contact, because he pulls himself even higher, his entire face pressed into my slit, the edge of his mask grazing my bottom. His tongue plunges deep into me again and he tilts his head, swirling the tip in teasing flicks, then pulling out again and shifting to my clit. I gasp and pivot my hips, giving him as much access as I can, and he takes the invitation, grasping my clit between his lips and sucking hard until I cry out.

"He's the best one yet, isn't he?" Percy murmurs, staring down at the chin between my thighs, which is all either of us can see of the man.

I can only manage a half-coherent "uh-huh" before the man shifts again, swiping his tongue back through my folds and continuing farther. He darts the quickest, lightest lick against my rear, which is just as exposed to him as the rest of me.

"Oh god. Oh, fuck!" I cry in a very un-queenly manner.

A devious chuckle comes from beneath me and his restraints creak again, his thighs flexing as he pushes himself farther below me. His tongue flicks teasingly around my asshole several times before he moves back to my pussy.

"Wish I could use my hands," he says in a low voice. "I'd make you come so fucking hard."

"N-No touching allowed," I stutter, too distracted by the image now stuck in my head of doing more with this man. Of feeling that thick shaft inside me, of riding him to completion. But his tongue is doing the job well enough on its own.

"I get it," he says, lips brushing in teasing caresses against my folds. "But I'd still be at your mercy. I would do whatever you asked me to do."

An idea springs to mind that gives me a vicarious thrill. Something I'm not willing to do myself, but that I know Percy might enjoy.

"Would you like to come when I do?"

He pauses his lazy licking and sucking for a moment, no doubt sensing it's a trick question. "I'd be a fool to turn down an orgasm, but I don't see you leaving that throne to give me one. What's the catch?"

I turn my head to face Percy, who still leans over my chair, gently cupping my breasts and pinching and rolling my nipples between thumbs and forefingers.

"My knight would do the honors, wouldn't you, Percival?"

Percy meets my gaze, studying me for a moment. If I could see his eyebrows, I imagine they'd be raised in surprise. We don't typically discuss our scenes after the fact, but when he was assigned as my bodyguard and assistant at the start of the year, the owner of Whitewood also provided me with a copy of his file.

He knows I know every detail about his sexual preferences. That he identifies as demisexual, someone who is only sexually aroused around partners they form an emotional bond with, but that he's also quite open to sex with any gender if the circumstances are right. And I remember another word in his file: *compersive*, which I admit I had to look up after reading it. It means he gains joy and arousal from seeing someone he cares about experience the same. We've never been intimate until tonight, but we've spent every waking hour together since I began this adventure. He moved into my guest room the first night and has been my shadow ever since. I hope it's worth the risk, but his silence makes me uncertain.

"If it's too much to ask…" I begin, and he shakes his head.

"Anything for you, my queen," he says, giving me a smile that assures me I haven't overstepped. "Provided your subject consents."

"Do you consent to allowing Percival to suck your cock?" I ask the man between my thighs.

He lowers to his headrest until all I feel are his even breaths cooling my hot, moist flesh. His cock still stands erect and weeping fluid from the tip, so the idea hasn't turned him off, but his silence stretches almost too long for comfort.

After a tense moment, he finally takes a breath and answers.

CHAPTER THREE

LANCE

*T*he only way to describe what I'm experiencing is sensory overload. My queen's pussy is still spread and glistening *right* above my face. Her clit is a swollen nub, the sensitive pink tip visible beneath its silken hood. I think this might be the first time I've ever seen a woman's pussy from this angle. It's a perfect pussy too, and studying it is certainly easier than the offer she just made me.

My cock doesn't seem to be the least bit shy about it, though, so I admit I have to sit with that realization for a minute before I answer. But I've wanted this woman since I set eyes on her at the start of the semester at Columbia. I struck fucking gold when I discovered she was a member of *the* most exclusive sex club in the state of New York—so exclusive I shouldn't even be here, but discovering a discarded invitation and sleuthing to find out what kind of party it was for was worth it, and even if I get caught and kicked out, it'll be a small price to pay for this moment of heaven.

But is getting my dick sucked by another man a price for being here? Or is it a bonus?

I know him too; the big blond guy is like her shadow. He goes wherever she goes on campus, and there's a pretty prevalent rumor among the other students that they're fucking. So it really wasn't a surprise at all that he'd also be her assistant here, even though his role is still not exactly clear. He's fully clothed, and I got the sense from her offer that touching her isn't something he usually does.

I don't believe either of them have recognized me, though. I don't sit in front of the lecture hall where Dr. Brennan teaches her Introduction to Women's and Gender Studies course. I sit near the back, usually next to one of the three other men who signed up for her class, and she pretty much *never* looks our way. The women in class all occupy the discussion well enough that I can just sit back and listen, and occasionally get annoyed at the one guy who likes to pipe up with some mansplainy nonsense every so often.

The mask I have on tonight helps, of course. I got fucking lucky sneaking in on what's apparently the Whitewood Club's monthly Masquerade Night, and managed to find a discarded mask within the rear stairwell. It smelled like coconut, but otherwise looked clean enough to serve my purposes.

And now here I am, marveling at the juiciest snatch I've ever seen, one I've fantasized about for months now, and only half-aware of the words already spilling from my lips.

"Only if you promise to let me make you come before I do."

What. The. Fuck. Did I just agree to let another man suck my dick?

I involuntarily clench my ass when he nudges my knees gently with the backs of his hands. The tension in my body must be obvious, because I hear her throaty chuckle above me.

"Relax. I don't *think* Percy will bite unless you ask him to."

I take a shuddering breath and peer down at him, which is a challenge, since I can't lift my head without sliding out from under her, and I'm not about to give up the best seat in the house just to get a better view of what he's up to.

Percy meets my gaze and offers the slightest smile, shaking his head. "I know what I'm doing. You don't have to worry."

I reluctantly part my knees and he settles between them, sitting back on his haunches, still fully dressed. He holds my gaze while he reaches back to pull his shoulder-length hair into a ponytail and secures it with an elastic from his wrist. The man is *prepared*.

A nervous laugh escapes me. "I guess I'm just worried I'm going to like it."

God, what an idiotic thing to say. I'm not a homophobe; I've just never thought about men *that way*. I focus on the reason I'm here again, because I'll be damned if I let myself get too distracted to follow through on my promise.

But not before he says in a low voice, "Would that be so bad?"

He rests both big, warm hands on my knees and gently slides them down my inner thighs, spreading my legs. I start tonguing the queen's snatch in earnest, gratified by the moan she lets out, but startled by a deeper moan coming from Percy when he takes my cock in hand and licks me from root to tip.

Time seems to slow in the next few moments, because I'm suddenly acutely aware of how little control I have over *anything*. That one lick was like a fuse being lit, and it's far shorter than I expected it to be.

When he wraps his lips around my tip and swallows me deeper than anyone ever has, it's all I can do to hold on. I go to town on the queen's pussy like my life depends on it, determined to get her there as promised. She starts rocking above me, her slick snatch a slippery feast for my senses. Then something unexpected happens.

She reaches down and covers my hands with her own where I'm clenching the handholds at the sides of her throne. I release my grip and spread my fingers, groaning in gratitude when she threads her fingers between mine and holds tight.

I'm not sure if I manage to get her there before I come, but she lets out a throaty cry after a moment and her pussy spasms, then utterly *drenches* my face. I go off like a goddamn rocket, but my tongue is somehow on autopilot, continuing to lap up all that delicious, tangy mess she just let loose.

Fucking hell, I thought squirting was a myth. I also thought what came out was something I'd rather not get all over me, but what I taste is the same slippery fluid I've been licking off her, just a *lot* more of it. And she keeps coming, her moans like music, her ass rocking above me, rubbing her core against my mouth.

Percy swallows every drop I shoot and slips his mouth off me, giving the tip of my dick a gentle kiss that sends a shiver up my spine. I want to look at him, but at the same time, I'm so focused on *her* I'd rather not let myself get distracted.

She hasn't told me to stop, so I don't. My jaw is starting to cramp, but I don't fucking care. I want her to remember me.

I'm losing circulation in my hands, she's holding on so tight, but her orgasms keep coming and coming. Finally her body shifts above me until I can't reach her with my mouth anymore, and she loosens her grip on my hands.

Breathlessly, she says, "You can stop now."

I let out a sigh and relax, working my jaw to ease its soreness as she scoots onto a narrow little ledge of a seat I hadn't realized was at the back of her throne. She peers down at me, her flush visible despite her dark complexion.

"Did I please my queen?" I ask, oddly compelled to remain formal despite what just occurred.

"Very much," she says with a smile. Her face lights up and my heartbeat stutters. Goddamn, could she be more beautiful? "In fact, I think you deserve a reward."

I blink up at her. "What you just gave me was the best reward I could ever ask for."

"Think about it. You have ten minutes to decide while we get cleaned up."

Percy appears at her side again, kneeling to unfasten one of my shackles before moving to the opposite side to take care of the other. He stands up and reaches his hand down to me. I grab it, appreciating the help up since my head is still spinning, and mindlessly accept the soft, moist cloth he hands me next. Curtains obscure the viewing window now that the show is over, As I clean myself up, I'm only abstractly aware that he isn't hard now, though I was sure I saw him sporting an erection through his pants just before he started sucking me off.

"How can you stand it?" I ask.

He lifts both eyebrows. "Stand what?"

"You didn't get to finish. That was so fucking hot. How can you stand being around a woman so beautiful when she's in the middle of ... *that*?" I wave my hand at the throne and the queen, who has repositioned her outfit so she's covered again. She looks as perfect as she did when I entered the room, though much more relaxed, and maybe even a little dazed and drunk. I can't help but smirk. *I* did that to her.

Percy shakes his head. "It takes a lot more to get me going to the point I don't want to stop. But she doesn't need a horny asshole as her bodyguard, so it works out well for us. I don't usually get hard at all during scenes with her. This was a first."

I cough a laugh. "Uh, should I be flattered?"

One blond eyebrow lifts and he chuckles. "If you want, but it wasn't you so much as how well you pleased *her* that turned me on. Seeing her get off is an aphrodisiac, and one of the few things that affect me that way."

This is a fascinating revelation, and not something I completely grasp. I'd like to know more, but the queen clears her throat. I redirect my attention to her and am dumbstruck yet again. I can't quite believe this happened.

"Have you thought about it?" she asks.

It comes to me that moment as I study her face, thinking about all the times I watched her standing at her podium in front of class, or pacing in front of the projector screen as she gives a lecture. I always fixate on her mouth, sometimes imagining her going down on me, but considering that's a dangerous fantasy to have in public, I mostly focused on what it would be like to simply kiss her.

"I know what I want," I say, moving close to face her once Percy repositions the backrest so it becomes her footrest again.

She gives me an expectant look, her eyes dark behind her mask. "I'm all ears."

"May I kiss you?"

Her eyelids flutter and her lips part, as if this was the last thing she expected me to say. After a beat, she stands. She's not a tall woman, her eyes barely an inch above mine where she stands on her throne's dais. She gives me a thoughtful look as she rests her hands on my shoulders, then steps off the dais. I take a step back to give her room, but she closes the distance.

"You may kiss me now," she says in a near whisper, looking up into my eyes.

I wish I could take off our masks. I want her to know who I am, to know she'll recognize me next Tuesday in class, but a kiss will have to be enough. I cradle her face in both hands, staring into her eyes for a breath before I lower my mouth to hers.

If I thought eating her pussy was enough to satisfy me, I was wrong. The kiss wakes up my every nerve and desire again. I will my dick to stand down so I can savor this, though, because this kiss isn't for me; it's for her. Because even if she can never know my identity, I want her to remember me.

CHAPTER FOUR

GWEN

I pass the next hour in a daze of afterglow, my body still alight and sensitive from *the* most mind-blowing climax I've ever had. That says something, considering I spend one night a month at this club seeking out orgasms. The rest of the month I try not to think about sex, because I want to get the most out of my escape into the persona of Queen Justine.

I can't stop thinking about him. He didn't lay a finger on me while he was pleasuring me, aside from clasping my hands, yet his tongue worked me over so well he didn't need to. But it wasn't until his last request that he really knocked me off-balance. A kiss should have been a simple thing to grant, but the moment his mouth pressed against mine, the moment his tongue gently probed between my lips and I let him in, I realized how much danger I was in.

Except for once it wasn't terrifying—it was exhilarating.

I play the moment over in my head while I sip hot tea in the sitting room downstairs. All the Whitewood Club's performers get together to unwind a little once the guests have departed. It's almost dawn, and I've been relaxing while

I listen to Brit and Casey gossip about one of their university professors, but I haven't joined in. I'm only half-listening anyway.

"I don't know, he just strikes me as the kind of perv who'd coerce sex out of a girl in exchange for a good grade," Casey says.

"Good thing we don't need help with our grades," Brit answers, then shivers a little.

"Has that ever happened to you, Gwen?" Casey asks. "I mean, has a student ever, um... *suggested* they'd offer sex in exchange for a good grade?"

I turn my attention to them, slow to find the thread of conversation.

"No, but two of them did invite me to a sex club. And no, it did *not* affect your grades, and you both know it."

Casey snorts a laugh. Brit cocks her head and studies me. "You seem different tonight. Are you feeling okay?"

"I feel fantastic," I say, unable to stop myself from smiling.

"Ooh, you got a good one tonight, didn't you? Do tell!" Casey says, setting down her tea and propping an elbow on one knee, chin against her palm. "I do miss the thrill of discovery, even though Rick and Max never cease to surprise me."

"Was it Percy?" Brit asks in an exaggerated whisper.

She glances toward the arched doorway but none of the men are nearby at the moment, since they oversee maintenance of the equipment at the end of every Masquerade Night. It's one of the few times I feel comfortable being away from Percy, but Brit and Casey are always good company.

I never would have imagined confiding in two female students about my attack would have paid off. All I told them was that I didn't feel safe anymore on campus and was considering resigning, since neither the administration nor the NYPD were doing much of anything to track down my attacker. The pair wouldn't hear of it, so they took it upon themselves to escort me in their downtime, and eventually offered to introduce me to someone who could help.

That was when I met Chloe, the proprietress of Whitewood, whose inviting manner coaxed the full story out of me, then presented several solutions. She assigned Percy to be my bodyguard right away, but the suggestion of reclaiming my power at the club one night a month wasn't something I entertained until later. After one visit as a guest, I saw the potential. Witnessing these two women more than ten years my junior enjoy themselves so thoroughly with men they trusted made me want to reclaim some of that joy, that *control*.

Because it wasn't lost on me how much power they had over the men who performed with them. They may have allowed themselves to be tied up and fucked, but the very second one of them used her safe word, the dynamic shifted; the men backed down, determined to ensure her safety and pleasure at all costs.

To be able to trust someone so much that a single word, or even a gesture, could control their partners' actions was something I realized I craved. So I made the hesitant suggestion to Percy, because by then his opinion mattered.

We eased into it at first on a slow night. Brit's partner in submission, Adam, volunteered to be my first subject, with Michael and Brit both in the room. At first I felt more like a prop in their fun, since Michael sat in a chair voicing subdued commands to the other two. He checked in with me at every step while Percy stood at my back.

Because I already trusted them it became fun and easy, and more than a little pleasurable, not to mention instructive. I learned what it means to be a dominant, and how crucial it is that my submissive's needs are met. Even though I'm here for my pleasure, their comfort is paramount.

Percy keeps me accountable, so I've learned to sense when my subject is enjoying themselves or not, but so far I haven't had to cut a scene short because they weren't.

"No, but Percy was more involved than usual tonight. I don't think it means anything."

"Oh, it does," Casey says. "Percy adores you."

"I think he also liked my subject, though, so what does that say?"

"Man or woman?" Brit asks.

"Man... one especially well-equipped in both tongue and dick."

Casey laughs, and Brit rolls her eyes at her friend. The pair are college roommates who act like sisters, though Casey is the more outspoken, adventurous one while Brit, daughter of a famous Broadway star—who once was a popular Domme at this club—is the delicate, deceptively angelic and brilliant beauty.

"Who knew Percy was bi?" Casey says when she regains her composure. "I have always wondered. He's so self-contained."

They evidently haven't been privy to his file, but it isn't my place to explain Percy's particular flavor of sexuality. Casey's comment about his feelings for me leaves a warm feeling in my belly. I kind of adore him too. Did my invitation to participate tonight really have more meaning to him than I thought?

The man in question appears while I'm pondering that, slipping silently into the room from a side door and coming up to my chair to squeeze my shoulder.

"You ready to go?" he asks.

"More than ready. I'm exhausted," I say. When I rise, he

takes the teacup from my hand and places it on a tray nearby, then grabs my jacket and holds it up for me to slip into. I catch Casey's single raised eyebrow and sly smile, as if she's silently telling me, *"See, I told you."*

I choose to ignore the suggestive look, because if it's true, I don't think I'm equipped to do anything about it anyway.

But it weighs on me when Percy brings the car around to the front and opens my door for me. He's always been a perfect gentleman, so I've always assumed his mannerisms were just him doing his job. Except the memory of his touch tonight slips unbidden into my mind—the way he pressed sensuous kisses to the side of my throat at my invitation, the way he reverently cupped and teased my breasts. My nipples harden at the thought, which spurs more memories from the night, of the other man and how delicious his tongue felt between my legs, of how eager Percy was to suck him off and how enthusiastically he carried out that task.

We arrive back at my brownstone and proceed with our usual routines like a married couple, except he slips into my downstairs guest room—which has been *his* room for months now—while I head up to my second-floor bedroom.

I lie awake for too long replaying the evening, aroused, yet disinterested in my vibrator, because I can't stop thinking of the very handsome, attentive man sleeping just below.

Heart in my throat, I slip out of bed and put on my robe, then quietly head downstairs.

CHAPTER FIVE

GWEN

*L*ight seeps from under Percy's door, so I knock lightly.

"Percy? Can we talk?"

He doesn't answer, but I hear footsteps, then the door swings open to reveal him wearing only a pair of flannel PJ bottoms. The aroma of spicy bodywash wafts off him, and for the first time ever, I'm overwhelmed by the sheer size and *maleness* of him. Somehow he's even bigger, half-dressed like this. He always remains fully clothed during our scenes.

"What's up?" he asks, his voice low as if afraid to wake someone up, even though we're the only ones here.

"I … um … can't sleep. I keep thinking about tonight. Can we talk about it?"

He regards me a second, then looks over his shoulder, hesitating. "Do you want to come in, or would you rather talk in the den?"

"In your room is fine," I say, not sure it matters where we have the conversation until I realize the only seating option in his room is on his bed, but it's too late now.

He gestures to the king-sized bed and I walk over,

climbing onto the end to face him while he sits against his pillows, knees bent with his forearms resting on top. I see a leatherbound journal splayed face-down on his bedside table, a pen on top.

"I didn't mean to interrupt. I figured you might be asleep."

"I don't sleep until you do."

"H-How do you know?"

He clears his throat and reaches for his phone. "It's only for your safety. You did give me permission in the contract you signed," he says, swiping to an app, then showing it to me. It looks like a fitness app, but I realize it has my name at the top and displays my sleep patterns going back several months. Ever since we first met.

"You've been spying on my sleep?" I'm incredulous, but he just shrugs and gives me a direct look.

"You know everything there is to know about me; I know Chloe shared my file with you. She shared yours with me too. You really should read the fine print of your contracts more carefully."

I vaguely remember a set of clauses that gave him permission to do what he saw fit to ensure my safety, within reason. It's weird, but oddly comforting knowing he takes his job seriously enough to go to these lengths.

I sigh and hand his phone back. "It's not an issue. But I want to make sure tonight isn't an issue for you. What I asked you to do... You could have said no."

"I didn't want to say no. Gwen, if you ever ask me to do something I don't want to do, I'll tell you. That's how these kinds of arrangements work."

"You make it sound like you're my submissive."

He lifts an eyebrow and smiles. "Aren't I?"

I open my mouth to respond, but find no words. Is he? Is that what this has been all along, with him tailing me like a puppy to ward off potential threats? To give me peace of mind?

Despite my monthly night of pleasure on the throne of Queen Justine, despite being trained for that role by a Dom, I have never thought of myself as one, but maybe that's exactly what I am.

"If you are, does the role extend outside of Whitewood?"

"This is a twenty-four-seven job for me. That's what we agreed on. I will do *anything* you ask, anything you need, anytime, day or night. So tell me what you need right now."

My mind spins. I'm afraid to voice the thing I *want*, opting to keep it tame for now and simply ask the question that's been plaguing me all evening.

"Do you want more from me than what we've had so far? More of a ... physical ... connection? After tonight, I couldn't stop wondering. I got the sense that you might have wanted it all along. That maybe you wanted to be where *he* was tonight."

His jaw clenches, his eyes going dark, then he takes a deep breath as if bracing himself.

"I need you to understand that my commitment to you involves putting your needs first, always. Asserting myself for my own pleasure isn't an option for me... not to mention it would wind up unsatisfying for us both if I did that. You did read my file, right?"

I nod, my stomach clenched at the unexpected honesty. He nods in return.

"Then you should know that at first, I didn't want anything more than to do my job. I enjoyed watching you come out of your shell more and more each month, but I was very aware when you hit your limit and it started to become routine. In all that time... in all the time we've spent together outside of Whitewood... I've grown to care for you very deeply. To the point that all it takes is to see you smile for me to get turned on."

My eyebrows rise at that. "Really? It's that easy?"

He chuckles. "It's fucking difficult as hell, because being aroused around you is distracting. It's safer at the club because I know nobody can get in who doesn't belong there. But when you invited me to participate tonight, there was no way I was going to turn you down.

"And to answer your question, yes, I'd have loved to be in your subject's place tonight. But watching you watch me pleasure him was almost as fun. Besides, he was doing such a good job I didn't want to make him stop just so we could share the honor."

Something inside me clenches tight at the very idea of *both* of them pleasuring me at the same time.

I catch another, more wicked smile stretch his lips, and he says, "I'm getting the impression you would have liked that, wouldn't you? Next time, don't hesitate to demand what you wish. The worst we could do is say no."

"*If* he ever returns, I'll try to remember that. We don't even know who he is," I say, forcing a smile through my bewilderment. I'm turned on now just thinking about it and pull my robe a little tighter, painfully aware of how hard my nipples are.

"I have a feeling he won't be able to stay away after that kiss. I don't think he was prepared to get sucked off by another man, if that says anything about how much he wanted to be there with his face buried in your pussy."

Another rush of endorphins floods me. "My word, you're always so buttoned up. How did I never know you had this side to you?"

"I'm just like you. It takes me a long time to trust someone enough to show them who I am. With you, I figured it was important to hold back until I thought you were ready for me to open up. Some people find it difficult to swallow exactly how I tick."

"Well, I for one really like how you tick. You're kind of perfect."

"As perfect as your masked lover tonight?" he asks with an arched eyebrow.

It's my turn to smile, because I can't quite believe how much he's revealed in only a few moments. But like he says, it takes time to trust, and I guess my coming to him today was what he needed to prove I was ready to see the real him.

"I really couldn't say who was more perfect. I've never spent time with him, obviously. And I've never been that intimate with you."

I'm dying for him to respond, but he merely nods. When the silence stretches, our gazes remain locked, and my heart beats so hard I can barely breathe.

He finally leans a little closer. "I'm not going to press. I will never initiate, because that would presume too much of someone I know isn't comfortable being on the receiving end of such assertiveness. Tell me what you want, Gwen."

This is so much harder than I expected, so I decide to start small, to test how just a tiny step toward intimacy will feel with him.

"I want what he asked for at the end. I want a kiss."

His eyes light up as if I've just offered him everything. "I think I can accommodate that," he says, then stretches out his legs and pats his flannel-covered thighs. "Take your time."

It's the closest to a command I think I've ever heard him give me. Even his instructions involving my security are always worded as suggestions, rather than orders, but I always defer to him when it comes to my safety.

I crawl farther up the bed and swing a leg over his, realizing too late how very wet I am. Even worse, I'm not wearing panties; the day after a Masquerade, my flesh is usually too sensitive to have anything rubbing against it.

But I decide I don't care whether he knows. He saw me lose myself to the abandon of multiple orgasms earlier. And I want very much to lose myself again with him.

CHAPTER SIX

PERCY

She's so close, so warm, so soft, it takes all my self-control to take things slow. But restraint is what makes everything taste even sweeter, so I obey my one rule with Gwen: always follow her lead when it comes to her body. I'm more assertive in public because she's adorably oblivious to her surroundings sometimes, so my higher level of environmental awareness means I'm often urging her in directions she might not want to go.

Once Chloe assigned me as Gwen's bodyguard, it only took a week for me to realize she probably needed a little nudge here and there to pay more attention. It also pisses me off that I couldn't have been there for her the night she was attacked. I don't blame her for it—none of it was her fault—but my desire to go back in time and stop it from happening never wanes.

Of course, it *did* happen, which is the only reason I'm here with her now. The only reason she's settling her soft backside against my thighs and scooting dangerously close to my crotch. She doesn't come all the way, but stops just before her pelvis can press against mine and rests her hands lightly on my shoulders. We're eye-to-eye and I watch her, waiting for her to take the lead, because this is what she needs to do to continue reclaiming her autonomy in a world that brutally stripped it from her.

"Is this okay?" she asks.

"You tell me."

She rolls her eyes a little. "Maybe I should rephrase... Is there anything you don't like about this?"

I smile. She's starting to get it. "Not a damn thing. I told you, you only need to ask."

She nods and takes a breath. "Put your hands on me, please. I don't want you to hold back, okay?"

"Noted," I say with a nod. "But you have to go first." I lift my hands off the bedspread and place them at her hips, squeezing gently to urge her on.

Our gazes lock and our breathing syncs, and for the first time since I've known her, I feel off-balance, suddenly uncertain whether I've made a terrible mistake letting her get this close. But before I can stop the whole thing from happening, she leans in, sliding her hands up my neck to bracket my jaw, just the way *he* did to her earlier. Then her lips press against mine, and I'm inexorably drawn under by the sweetness of her kiss.

She moans a little against my mouth and some deep, needy part of me responds. I slide my hands up her sides, then around her back and pull her tighter. Almost immediately warm wetness soaks through my pajamas, and the acute awareness of her arousal—and the fact that she's probably been this way during our entire conversation—sends my own desire into the stratosphere.

There's no controlling my cock now that she's pressed against it, and I swallow the sudden gasp she lets out when she feels my hardness pressing against her soaked flesh. She grinds against me and I moan again, head starting to spin from the rush of sensation.

"Percy..." she whines. "I need you to touch me."

"I would fucking *worship* you, if you'd let me," I murmur, sliding my lips across her jaw and down her throat. I grasp the collar of her robe and the strap of her flimsy nightgown and tug them off her shoulder, trailing my lips and tongue along her silken skin.

She tilts back with a sigh, letting me support her with my other arm while I explore with my mouth, the angle creating more friction between her pussy and my dick. Her nightgown is made of a soft, stretchy fabric and gives easily when I tug, one breast coming free, revealing a dark nipple as hard as a diamond. I wrap my lips around it and suck, reveling in her desperate moan. She grinds harder against me, my pajamas soaked through from her arousal.

"I need to feel you," she says, slipping one hand down my belly to tug at the drawstring of my pants.

"Please let me taste you first," I say, pulling back to look into her eyes.

Her gaze is feverish with desire, but she gives me a slight smirk. "Feeling a little competitive, are we?"

I laugh. "Yes and no. I wanted to fuck him as much as I wanted to *be* him and prove to you that I could give as good as he did."

Her mouth falls open. "That's really hot. Watching you make him come was hot too. I can't stop thinking about it."

My nostrils flare at the knowledge that she's been fantasizing about watching me go down on our guest tonight. It makes me want to find the guy so we can repeat the experience and do *all* the things she really wishes we'd done. But Masquerade Night is all about anonymity, so it's unlikely Chloe would give us his identity.

I grip her hips and tilt mine up, grinding hard against her. Her swollen clit is evident, a firm bud rubbing along the underside of my dick.

"Don't move from this spot," I say, gripping her hips and urging her to rise. Then I dig my heels into the mattress and haul myself straight down between her legs until I'm right where I want to be. She shrugs out of her robe and tears her nightgown off, leaving her delightfully naked above me. Her midnight waves frame her face as she stares down at me, then tenderly combs her fingers through my hair.

I pull her down, right onto my mouth, saliva already pooling before her silken flesh meets my tongue. The second I wrap my lips around her clit, she throws her head back with a moan.

I know it isn't a competition, but my lizard brain would love nothing more than to make her come as hard as he made her come tonight, just to know what it feels like when she lets loose.

Unlike him, I have the benefit of being able to use my hands, so I do, sliding one across her thigh to spread her folds wide while I press the fingers of my other hand into her channel, sliding through the wetness until I find her opening. I push two fingers into her and start gently fucking while I suck and flick her clit with my tongue. She clings to my head at first, then leans backward and props her hands on my hips behind her. She undulates in time with my fingers moving in and out, her moans rising in volume and her movements speeding up.

She's so fucking close I can taste the flood on the verge of breaking. It takes only a moment more before her muscles clamp tight around my fingers and the first spurts of tangy fluid rush across my tongue. Then an entire flood comes, filling my mouth and dripping down my chin, and I'm so fucking turned on I could probably come from a light breeze.

She moans and shudders, but before I regain my senses, she moves down my body, a wild look in her eyes.

"I want you inside me," she says, and by then I'm so dumbstruck I don't have enough functioning brain cells to decide whether that's a good idea. But it feels better than good when she shoves my waistband down, grips my cock, and presses my tip to her entrance.

Her wetness cools on my cheeks, but I'm too absorbed in watching my dick disappear into her tight heat to care. I just grab her hips and hold on, mesmerized by how fucking beautiful she is in this moment and how amazing she feels wrapped around me.

She stares down at me with a smile. "You are covered in me. You liked being smothered by my pussy, didn't you?"

"Fucking loved it. Anytime you want a face to sit on, all you have to do is ask, my queen."

She throws her head back with a breathy moan, bouncing her entire body on top of my dick. I can't help myself, so I reach up and cup her breasts, overwhelmed by the privilege that I get to be the one to share this with her, to share the moment she finally grasped how much power she could have over a man.

I can't imagine she can come again, but she does only moments later, which is all it takes for me to let loose as well. The world spins on its axis when our cries mingle and her pussy clamps tight around my cock. Every nerve ending in my body comes alive with pleasure, and when she leans over and kisses me again, I latch on, hungry for every ounce of attention she's willing to give.

We keep kissing until our heartbeats slow and my cock

softens inside her, but she remains splayed atop my chest, breathing rough and ragged.

"I needed that," she says, then turns to rest her chin on her hands and look into my eyes. I still have no words, so I just lift both eyebrows. Then she adds, "I think you needed it too. God knows you earned it."

"I'm only entitled to whatever attention you choose to give me. It feels good to be chosen, though."

She lifts her head, frowning. "You're a catch, Percy. I've monopolized your time for the better part of a year now, but never thought to ask about your love life. Or your social life, for that matter. Is there more to you besides working at Whitewood and being my bodyguard?"

"Does there need to be?" I ask, unsure whether I'm ready to go that deep with her. We've kept things professional until tonight, which means our conversations have always remained pretty formal too. The trust she has for me grew out of action, not words, and I've been grateful that she never dug deeper.

She studies me in silence for a moment, then presses her lips tighter together and shakes her head. "You don't have to tell me anything you don't want to, but it won't stop me from wanting to know more. I get that just because a physical barrier has been broken between us doesn't mean an emotional one will follow. But I genuinely like you—probably more than like—but I think we both know anything deeper requires deeper trust."

I lift a hand to brush a strand of dark hair off her forehead, letting out a slow breath. "It isn't lack of trust that holds me back so much as a sense of duty. At Whitewood, you learn to separate the physical from the emotional if you want to get the most out of the experience, but I don't work that way. I care about you. If I didn't, tonight would have never happened. I'd never have participated in the scene, and I definitely would have told you to go back to bed when you came to my door. If I don't hold *something* back, I'll lose myself, and I'd be a pretty shitty bodyguard if I let that happen."

"You have to keep one foot on the ground, is that what you're saying?"

"Exactly."

Her gaze tracks mine, but something in the new connection we just formed feels like it falters. She gives a short nod, then sighs as she slides off me. It's all I can do not to reach for her and pull her back onto me, but she's already up, slipping back into her nightgown and robe. A knot forms in my chest as I watch her put herself back together, her expression shuttered.

I've fucked up, but I'm not sure if I can fix it. Still, I yank my pajamas up again, then sit up and swing my legs off the side of the bed, reaching for her hand.

"You don't have to go."

Her eyebrows draw together and she emits a bitter laugh. "Don't I?" Then she clenches her eyes shut and heaves a breath. "Fuck, I hate how I sound. I'm not mad at you. Just…"

"Disappointed."

"Yeah," she says. She looks resigned now, her shoulders sagging. She forces a smile, then and bends down to kiss me on the forehead. "Which I know is unfair to you, but it'll pass."

I slip my arms around her waist and pull her close, reveling in the way she holds my head against her chest, gently carding her fingers through my hair. If she had *any* clue how much I need exactly this, I fear she'd lose all respect for me, but I let myself savor the moment because I'm pretty sure she just lied to me. I had my chance, and I blew it because I was unwilling to really open up.

After too short a time, she pulls away, and I reluctantly let her go. She doesn't look back as she opens the door, walks through, and closes it gently behind her. I stare at it for ages after she's already gone.

CHAPTER SEVEN

LANCE

*D*r. Brennan is as stunning as ever at Tuesday's Intro to Women's and Gender Studies class, but something seems off.

It takes me the first fifteen minutes of her lecture to realize the easy familiarity that once existed between her and her assistant is gone. They both look tense, but Percy's just as watchful as ever, though rather than his constant scanning of the students, I catch him staring at *her* most of the class. Once I even catch him blink and shake his head, mouthing a silent curse that I doubt he thinks anyone sees.

I'm usually transfixed by her alone, but ever since I happened upon the pair of them in a very unexpected locale over the weekend, I've been more than curious about them both. I suppose it stands to reason that after a guy sucks your dick, you *might* want to know a little more about him too.

The club was a discovery of a lifetime by itself, though, something I stumbled upon by accident that opened my eyes to a whole new world of adventure I never even considered I might be into.

Casey and Brit, two of the girls who live at Woodbridge

Hall where I do, were dressed for a formal Saturday night, and one of them dropped an invitation on her way through our residence hall lobby. I picked it up, thinking I might actually have a fun weekend diversion instead of just studying or training for my next swim meet.

Except there was no address on the thing.

But I'm resourceful. It took quite a bit of internet searching, but I finally found myself in the ballpark. Most of what I found about Whitewood Club was from a smutty romance novel that features the place, but evidently the author is also a member who lives nearby. She wrote it as if it was made up, which most of the info online suggests is true—that it's pure fiction—but the fancy engraved invitation I found suggested otherwise.

I wound up borrowing my rich roommate's car and driving to one of the swankiest neighborhoods outside the city, where every property sits behind a wall with a dedicated guard at the gate. One in particular had two cars waiting for entry. Since I had the invite in hand, I took a chance and pulled in right behind the second car. To my surprise, the guard actually let me through.

When I parked and realized everyone heading inside was wearing a mask, I wasn't sure what I'd do, so rather than enter through the front, I snuck around in the shadows to the back of the house where I found a staff entrance. All the staff wore black dress clothes, and I was fortunate to be wearing black jeans and a black T-shirt, so I blended enough to go unnoticed.

I headed for a stairwell, stopping inside when I heard the unmistakable sounds of a pair of people passionately screwing on the landing. Rather than interrupt, I waited, and moments later a man and woman rushed by and out the exit.

I found both their discarded masks on the landing, snagged one, and put it on.

I'm not sure what I expected, but definitely *not* a full-on sex club complete with viewing rooms where couples and trios—and more—were performing for an enraptured audience. Everyone was wearing colored arm bands, though, and I wanted to blend in. After wandering around the second floor for a bit, I finally found a counter near an elevator with an array of ribbons hanging on the wall behind a voluptuous woman in a striped satin corset.

"What's your flavor tonight, sir?"

"I'm not sure what I'm in the mood for." It was an honest reply. The whole scene was a little overwhelming, and I'd been fighting a hard-on since I walked in.

She gave me an understanding nod, then handed me a laminated menu. An actual *menu*. Except the items listed weren't food, but *kinks*. Or rather, a variety of sexual acts and fetishes. I tried not to gawk and scanned it like it was just an average night out for me.

"I think I'll keep it simple tonight. Light blue."

She reached for a light blue roll of ribbon and snipped off a length. "Nothing wrong with that. Giving or receiving?"

Both, I thought, but since I was just dipping my toes in, I figured I'd be less likely to blow my cover if I wasn't just taking.

"I'm a giver," I said with a grin.

She laughed. "That's what I thought. Left arm, please."

She hummed in appreciation when she gripped my bicep so she could secure the ribbon around it, then patted me gently on the shoulder and winked. "Have fun tonight."

I headed back the way I'd come, people-watching as I meandered. Most of the partygoers were in formal wear, but not all, so I didn't feel too out of place with the mask and ribbon. I didn't see the two girls from my dorm among them, which was probably fortunate, because there's a chance they would have recognized me even with the mask.

Every room had a large window for viewing the performance going on within. One contained a naked, masked woman trussed up in ropes with two men circling her, touching and teasing. I stood at the back of the onlookers and watched for as long as I dared, because it was so goddamned hot it was better than watching porn. Probably because this girl actually looked like she was enjoying being lightly whipped with a leather flogger while clamps were attached to both her nipples and labia.

She slowly rotated in her bindings, and when she turned to face the window again, I did a double-take. It was *Casey*. Holy motherfucking fuck. That was when I turned on my heel and moved on, hoping my eyes hadn't popped too far out of their sockets, not because I didn't want to watch, but I didn't want to risk being recognized.

But the next room held a similar shock, because within it, Brit was on her knees beside her boyfriend Adam, both naked and bound with collars around their throats while a man in a tuxedo murmured low commands to them, which they enthusiastically obeyed.

I nearly choked when Brit buckled on a strap-on harness while Adam went down on hands and knees, but recovered with no more than a soft cough into my fist. A nearby woman turned to look at me, then scanned me from head to toe, gaze lingering on my armband before drifting to my mouth.

I turned away quickly, moving on and hoping the next room didn't contain anyone I actually knew. I was not so lucky.

I have zero regrets, except for the fact that I can't stop

thinking about both my teacher and her assistant now. I get hard remembering the taste of her, but the memory of the blowjob he gave me puts every other blowjob I've ever gotten to shame.

By the time class is over, I've barely taken any notes, so I'm glad I recorded the day's lecture to listen to later. Hopefully the sound of Dr. Brennan's voice doesn't set me off as much as looking at her does.

I wait a few moments for other students to leave, giving myself a chance to cool down before I stand. I'm packing my notebook into my backpack when I overhear a couple of the dudebros at the back of the lecture hall chatting.

"I heard someone broke into her office a few months back and assaulted her. That's why she's got that muscle-head shadow now."

"No shit?" another says. "Like, as in *sexual* assault?"

My nostrils flare and I go still, glancing over at them. There are three guys who I recognize as members of the golf team—a bunch of privileged white assholes.

"Not sure, but she didn't look injured or anything in class the week after, so probably," the first guy says.

They push through the doors as they talk, and I fall into step right behind, glaring at the backs of their heads, but not engaging. Is what he said true?

The third guy snickers and mutters something I don't quite hear. His friend shoots him a warning look. "Dude, you can't fucking say shit like that."

"What? You know I'm right. Don't tell me you wouldn't hit an ass that fine." He makes a lewd motion with his hands in front of his hips, pivoting his pelvis.

Rage colors my vision. I drop my bag and grab the back of his collar, slamming him face-first into the wall.

CHAPTER EIGHT

LANCE

*D*udebro grunts and cranes his neck, giving me a wild look out of one eye. "What the fuck?" he yells in a shrill, terrified voice.

I stick my nose against his ear. "You'd better watch your fucking mouth about Dr. Brennan, asshole, or I'll break all your goddamn teeth." I haul him back and slam him against the wall again, gratified by the smear of blood that colors the beige paint from his busted lip.

His friends catch up to us, and one yells, "Get the fuck off him!"

The other guy grabs my shoulder and I spin, fist swinging. I'm ready to lay them all out if I have to, but this one is a hefty guy, so my punch hits his fleshy gut without doing much to stop him. He grapples me and shoves. I shove back and he twists one hand into the back of my collared shirt, swinging a meaty fist into my kidney. The pain throws me off-balance and he pushes me the rest of the way over, the soft fabric of my shirt tearing from the collar down as I drop. I fall under his weight with a pained grunt as his knee lands against my groin. Not a direct hit to my balls, but close enough to hurt like a motherfucker.

The other two are above me then. The one I bloodied lands a kick to my side while the other bends over and swings at my face. I don't dodge fast enough and his knuckles glance off my mouth, pain slicing through my lip.

I kick and squirm, but the big guy has me pinned to the floor by the shoulders while the others wail on me. Another kick, another fist to the face. My rage is the only thing keeping me numb to the pain.

"What're you, a fucking pussy-licking teacher's pet?" the bloody one sneers.

I grin through body-wracking agony and blood, ready with a retort that would've probably made me just as bad as them. Before I can get it out, a big hand grabs the upper arm of the guy pinning me and throws him off me.

Percy appears in his place, his sheer size enough to make the other two guys scramble back in fear.

"Get the fuck out of here before I call campus security," he snaps without even raising his voice. All three of them grab their forgotten backpacks and sprint away.

Percy reaches a hand out to me, and I grip it and let him haul me up. A bizarre sense of déjà vu hits at the parallel to the other night, when he helped me up after I'd had my tongue buried in Dr. Brennan's pussy for half an hour or more. My dick stirs, and I'm grateful for the throb of pain that settles it down.

I lift the hem of my shirt to dab at my bloody lip, find even more blood gushing from my nose, and wince. Percy reaches into his lefthand pocket and hands me a pristine powder-blue hanky that inspires yet another flashback to Saturday night. Light blue worn on the left means you're into giving oral sex. It didn't hit me until now that I could've been offering myself to men as well as women.

I stare at it for a beat as that sinks in before he lifts it up. "You're bleeding like a stuck pig, in case you haven't noticed."

I finally take the hanky and press it to my mouth, then hold it against my nose with a muffled, "Thanks."

Percy nods and tilts his head. "Come on. I think there's some ice and a First Aid kit in the lounge. I'll get you cleaned up, though I don't think there's any helping that shirt."

I crane my head to look over my shoulder. This was a new shirt, one of few button-downs I own. A draft wafts across my upper back where the seam has torn. "As long as the fashion police don't see me, I'll survive."

"I might have a spare I can loan you," he says. He turns to head down the hall and I follow, too dazed by the turn of events to do anything else.

"Do I even want to know what that was about?" he asks in the same soft-spoken tone he used at the club.

"Just defending Dr. Brennan's honor is all. They said some things that I hope aren't true about her."

His jaw spasms and he glances at me warily. "Tell me."

I get the sense this guy is ex-military, which should have been evident all along, if I'd paid any attention to him until now. His watchful posture and how he plants himself in a corner of the lecture hall with a view of all the doors should be a dead giveaway.

I grunt and shake my head. "Let me stop bleeding first, if that's okay."

He directs me into a staff lounge and pulls a chair out from one of the tables, then goes rifling through the cabinets. He returns a minute later with a First Aid kit and starts by unceremoniously tilting my head back and shoving cotton balls up my nostrils.

"Jeez, I'm not just a piece of meat here," I protest.

"Tell me what they said." He pauses long enough to look into my eyes, and I know he's going to keep at me until I give in.

"That Dr. Brennan was attacked. Sexually assaulted. Then one of them said something I'd rather not repeat, and that's when I lost my shit."

He utters a soft curse and shakes his head. He reaches for a sterile wipe and grips my jaw, dabbing the alcohol-infused cloth to my split lip. I wince, but look into his eyes.

"Is it true? Did someone attack her? They said that's why you're here. You're not just her TA, are you?" It's a dumb question, considering what I know, but he doesn't need to know what I know.

"It's no one's business. You shouldn't have gotten involved."

"It's a little late for that. Tell me I didn't get a black eye and probably some broken ribs for nothing."

He gives a wry smirk. "They deserved it. Let me take a look at your ribs, see what the damage is."

"Are you a doctor? Maybe I'd rather keep my shirt on."

"Former Navy medic. You'll at least want to ice it, if not wrap it soon. You're on the swim team, right? It's going to slow you down as it is, but will for a lot longer if you don't take care of it."

"Fine." I relent and start unbuttoning my shirt while he heads to the freezer and grabs an ice pack. I thought he was prepared with a hair tie the other night, but I had no idea.

I slip out of my shirt and hold it up to inspect the damage. Maybe I can get it repaired, or just survive without an extra dress shirt. Most of the students at this university are upper-class spoiled brats who didn't get the grades for Ivy League, but I'm on scholarship, so I don't exactly have a lot of spare cash to throw around.

When I drop the shirt to my lap, Percy freezes a few feet away, staring at me in shock. Or rather, at my upper arms—my tattoos.

"Ah, fuck," I mutter.

"Percy?" comes a familiar female voice from the hallway, then the door opens behind me and my spine tingles at Dr. Brennan's very presence. She's breathless, her tone agitated, on the verge of panicked. "Percy! Chloe just called. She says there was a security breach at the club Saturday night. Did you notice anything off? We need to go back out there this afternoon and watch the security footage. What if he was there? What if he got through and came after me?"

I don't dare turn around. Instead I watch Percy look from me to her, then back to me. I know the moment she registers my presence and sees my back. I won't get up, because I'm pretty sure Percy would put me back down, and not in a nice way, so I just turn, and the absolute fear in Dr. Brennan's eyes breaks my heart.

"Oh god. Oh god, no. It was you."

CHAPTER NINE

GWEN

My stomach drops when I see the top half of a tattoo I recognize on the back of the man in the chair. I freeze, staring at Percy in disbelief.

"Please, no. Please tell me it wasn't him."

Percy squares his shoulders and closes the distance to me, shooting *him* a warning glance as he passes. The man in the chair looks worried when he turns his head, and he should.

When Percy reaches me, he grips both my shoulders and looks into my eyes. "Gwen, it wasn't him. He's not the man who attacked you."

"H-How do you know?"

He huffs a breath through his nose and glances back at the other man. "Believe it or not, this guy got that bloody nose by defending your honor. He seems to like winding up on his back."

I stare at the bruised and bloody face, distorted by the cotton stretching both his nostrils. He's still craned around to watch, eyes wide like he's waiting for the other shoe to drop. Some of the coiled tension in me eases. Cautiously I walk around the chair to face him.

My subject.

My *student.*

"You're Lance Lacosta from my Intro to Women's and Gender Studies class. You always sit in the back of class with those other... *boys.*"

"They aren't my friends, if that's what you're thinking," he says.

"Did they do this to you?" I've endured the leering looks of those particular students all semester, but Lance has always stood apart. It's a relief to know he doesn't associate with them.

He nods, and I wince as I take in the split lip and darkening bruises spreading beneath his eyes. One side of his well-muscled torso is red and beginning to purple.

"Percy, give me the ice."

Percy shakes his head. "I'll take care of it. We can deal with the breach later. I'll meet you back in your office."

Despite solving the mystery of who breached security at the club, I'm not prepared to head back to my office alone just yet. "I'll wait. I want to talk to him."

Percy looks miffed, but shakes his head. "Fine, but this isn't really the place to have the conversation I think you want to have right now."

Lance is watching me rather than Percy when Percy squats beside him and presses the ice pack to his bruised side. He jerks at the shock, but doesn't look away from my face. He looks like he's holding his breath.

"Hand me the bandage. We need to wrap this," Percy says. I grab the rolled up athletic bandage, but rather than hand it to him, I unclip the metal holder and kneel in front of Lance to start binding the ice pack to his side. He stares at me in disbelief.

"Why did this happen?" I ask.

When he finds his voice, he says, "They were rumor-spreading dicks. Said awful things about you. I just couldn't let it slide."

"What did they say?"

He frowns and looks at Percy for guidance.

Percy sighs and shakes his head. "Sounds like word somehow got out about what happened to you last October. I suppose we're lucky it took as long as it did."

I tense and my hands start to shake, but I will myself to keep them steady while I bind this poor boy's ribcage. *Boy? Can you really think of him that way after Saturday?*

Percy watches me for a moment, then says, "I'm going to go grab him a clean shirt. Will you be okay for a few?"

"I'll be fine," I say.

Percy nods, then hands Lance a second icepack. "For your face." Then he shoots Lance a warning look and leaves the lounge, closing the door behind him.

I'm hyperaware of how intently Lance watches me, but despite this odd turn of events, I don't feel unsafe with him.

Taking a breath, I ask, "How old are you?"

"Twenty-one. I hope I didn't break any laws the other night."

"Depends. Did you break and enter?"

"Nope, just walked through an unlocked back door."

"Why were you even there? Who told you about the club?"

"No one. I found an invitation to a party in the lobby of my residence hall. Thought it sounded fun. I had no idea what to expect. No idea *who* I'd see. Is it true what they said?"

His abrupt question catches me off-guard, and it takes a second for me to figure out he's not talking about the club, but about the rumor that instigated his fight.

I glance up from my task and meet his eyes. He has a deep

furrow between his eyebrows, and I get the sense he wants me to tell him no. When I just drop my gaze again, he curses.

"I'm going to fucking kill them," he mutters.

I jerk my gaze back up. "No, you will not. Those idiots had nothing to do with it. Just leave it alone."

"Who did it?" he demands.

I fasten the bandage, but don't have the strength to stand again. I reach for a chair and drag it over, then rise and sit, closing my eyes against the nausea that roils in my belly.

"I don't know," I whisper. "I never saw his face. He was fast, strong. He came up behind me in my office when I wasn't looking, grabbed my hair, forced me to my knees, blindfolded me, then…" I take a shuddering breath, not quite believing I'm explaining all this, but unable to stop. "Then he forced me to open my mouth…"

The moment rushes back in an icy, terrifying flood. The shock of it, the paralyzing fear, then not being able to breathe because he'd shoved himself down my throat. The panic, then the surrender. I still hate myself for not fighting harder.

A warm hand squeezes my knee, then grips one of my forearms where I have them wrapped tight around my belly.

"You don't have to keep talking," Lance says. "I won't hurt you."

I take a breath and open my eyes, finding the will to smile when I see the deep concern etched on his bruised face. It's a little comical with his cotton-stuffed nostrils, which helps diminish the power of the memory that had me in its grip.

"I wasn't worried about you," I say. "I wouldn't have let Percy leave if I was. And he wouldn't have left if he didn't trust you. He's usually a better judge of character than I am."

I glance at the door, belly roiling for another reason now. Percy and I have barely spoken since I left his bedroom the morning after the Masquerade. I know I'm the one who needs to bridge the chasm between us, but I'm not quite sure how, not as long as he's holding back. I know I can trust him with my safety, but we started down a path with too many barriers to trust for things to end any way but badly.

"Do the cops have any idea who did it? They have security cameras in this building, don't they? Surely they could find him."

"They did the bare minimum, and that's it. I'm not holding my breath. It isn't your concern."

That earns me a pained look, and he swallows and turns away. His jaw spasms, and I'm briefly struck by how very handsome he is without a mask covering the top half of his face. He has thick, dark lashes that frame hazel eyes, an odd combination with his otherwise Latino features. I have the strangest urge to reach out and caress the contour of his strong cheekbone.

When he turns back, he has a determined set to his jaw. "If they won't find him, I will." The flash of fury betrays the intent he doesn't speak—that he'd probably kill the bastard for me, if he could only learn his identity.

"Lance, no. I just want to move on. The club is helping me do that. What I do there has done more to help me reclaim my power than finding my attacker ever could."

"But you still don't feel safe here. That's not fucking cool. And what if you weren't the only woman he did that to?"

I blanch at that thought. He's right, but if I let myself think about it, I won't even be able to function.

"I'm sorry," he says, "and I know it's none of my business, but the thought of you being hurt that way…" He struggles for more, but eventually settles on a frustrated curse.

"I appreciate the concern, really." I smile, genuinely

comforted by his outrage, and reach for his hand. He takes my hand and squeezes, studying my face.

"You're so fucking beautiful," he says in a hushed tone so blatantly honest and uncensored I blush. I retrieve my hand and resist the urge to avert my eyes from his. But our last encounter empowers me.

"You're not so bad yourself, aside from the obvious." I make a circular gesture indicating his face.

He chuckles and grabs the roll of paper towels Percy left on the table, then rips one off and holds it over his face, carefully removing the cotton from his nose. He dabs gently at his nose, which has stopped bleeding, but the bruises beneath his eyes have gone a deep shade of purple and blood still tinges his teeth.

"I wish this wasn't how we were first properly introduced. Please tell me you're turned on by the rough look."

I tilt my head as I study his mouth, for the first time very aware of how skilled he was with it the other night. His nervous laugh is deep and sexier than I think he realizes. I momentarily forget who we are, and *where* we are, as our gazes lock. The moment stretches, charged with what I know we're both thinking. But Percy returns, and the noisy din of students in the corridor outside yanks me back to the present.

"Sorry, it's all I've got," Percy says, handing Lance a rolled-up T-shirt while giving me a suspicious look.

Lance heaves a shaky breath and accepts the proffered shirt, shaking it out. "Dude, are you fucking with me? You *want* me to get beat up again, right?" He gives Percy an incredulous look.

I frown and he turns the powder-blue shirt around. A pink cartoon pony frolics across the front. Above it arches the words, "Free Pony Rides."

A laugh bubbles up and I can't contain it. "Oh, Percy. Really?"

"Just keeping him humble," he says with a smirk.

Lance pulls the shirt over his head, which ironically fits. He turns and gives me a faux smile. "If I don't make it to class on Thursday, you'll know who to blame."

CHAPTER TEN

GWEN

*L*ance is back in class looking no worse for wear on Thursday. His bruises cause several of the young women in class to stare at him, and rather than sit near the frat boys in the back, he parks himself front and center five full minutes early. The young woman who usually has that spot looks pissed when she finds him there and is forced to find another seat.

I shouldn't encourage him, but I return his smile. He shoots a look over his shoulder at the trio who beat him up and flips them the finger. When Percy is prepping handouts, Lance volunteers before any of the usual helpers to distribute them. Since my class is an elective for most of the students, I have a mix of ages, but the vast majority who take the class are women. Half of them track him around the room, every bit as interested as they usually are in Percy. It's probably because his bruises are even more shocking today, having turned a deep shade of purple. But a pang of jealousy hits unbidden and lingers throughout the ninety-minute lecture.

I'm in my office after class with the door open when a knock sounds. I look up to see Lance leaning on the jamb with a smile that makes my pulse speed up. Percy appears at his shoulder, looking irritated.

"She's busy. In the future, see me before you come bother her, got it?"

"It's okay, Percy. What's up, Mr. Lacosta?"

"I just wanted to see if there's anything I can help with. Maybe give that cranky cocksucker a little break or something." He jabs his thumb over his shoulder at Percy, who is still standing six inches behind him.

Percy scowls. "That language is unnecessary."

I raise my eyebrows. I never knew Percy to be such a prude about foul language, but I suspect there's more to his irritation than that. Jealousy, maybe? Which should be concerning, if it's true.

Lance smirks back at him. "By the way, I'm keeping the shirt. You would not believe the number of honeys who flirted with me on my way back to my dorm the other day. Not that I was interested."

He returns his gaze to me, and that million-watt smile is back.

Before I can respond, he says, "I don't have to take his job, though. I can do any task you need. And I mean *anything*."

The subtext is not lost on me, and my body warms at the implication.

"Okay, that's enough," Percy says, grabbing Lance's arm and hauling him out of my doorway. "You can't talk to her that way, idiot. In case it's lost on you, you're a student. She's your *teacher*. She could lose her job if the dean got wind of anything."

"Percy!" I snap. "Not in the hallway. Both of you come in and shut the door. We need to talk."

Percy switches directions, pulling Lance into my office and shoving him into a chair on the other side of my desk before closing the door. He leans against it, glaring at the back of Lance's head.

I heave a sigh. "He's right, Mr. Lacosta. I need you to stop whatever you're doing. The ass-kissing is going to raise red flags."

His eyebrows shoot up. "You do realize that everyone already thinks the two of you are screwing, right?" He twists around and glances at Percy before looking back at me.

It's my turn to be surprised. "No, I hadn't realized. Did you know?" I direct the question to Percy, who shakes his head.

"Is it true?" Lance asks.

"I…" I trail off, giving Percy a helpless look. He just stares at me as if daring me to come clean.

My hesitation is enough for Lance to fill in the blanks. "I see," he says, deflating a little. "But he barely touched you on Saturday. And then after … well, after what he did to me, I kind of assumed…"

"You assumed wrong," Percy says. "But we only made love once."

Lance turns again and stares at Percy for several seconds. "I'm sorry, man. That must hurt."

Percy clenches his jaw. "It's really none of your business."

His pained look sends a slice of regret through me, but he doesn't meet my gaze. We *need* to have a conversation soon.

"Well, considering we've all been up close and personal in each other's *business*, it's at least somewhat of interest," Lance says.

"It's between me and Percy," I interject. "But you're right about one thing: We need to discuss your *visit* to Whitewood on Saturday."

Percy stands up straighter. "Gwen, should we really do this here? The club would be the better venue."

"If you're concerned, lock the door and pull the blinds. I don't think this should wait."

He looks like he might challenge my decision, but after a beat relents and turns the deadbolt, then lowers the blinds that cover the sidelight, then the ones at the window overlooking the quad two stories below.

"Shit." Lance slouches in his seat, looking chagrined. "How badly did I fuck up?"

"Considering no one else came into contact with you at the club, it could be worse. But Whitewood is very strict about who they allow in. Everyone has to undergo full blood panels. Birth control methods are enforced as well, in situations where intercourse might occur. Condoms are optional at the club."

Lance absorbs this, then swallows and nods. He looks back at Percy. "I get tested before every meet—one of the perks of being on a swim scholarship for an NCAA school." His tone is tinged with irony, so I gather he doesn't particularly like the invasiveness of the testing. "And I'm not exactly promiscuous. No fucking time, if I want to graduate next year."

The corner of Percy's mouth twitches. "No *fucking* time..."

Lance chuckles. "I knew you had a sense of humor. How could you survive being so close to her all the time without one?"

"Can you get the results of your last test?" I ask. "I smoothed things over with the club's owner, but the blood test would ease everyone's minds." I glance at Percy, whose attention is fixed on Lance with much less animosity than before.

Looking at Lance again, I continue. "Since your visit to Whitewood was restricted to room fourteen, I asked Chloe to let me handle it. We don't like getting authorities involved because it invites undesired scrutiny, despite the fact that no money exchanges hands and illicit substances are forbidden."

Lance nods and pulls out his phone. "I have a copy in my email. I can send it over now." He taps a few times, glancing up while he completes the task. "So... what if I wanted to come back this weekend to see you? Assuming I'm only allowed to service the *queen*, and not, you know... *you*, Dr. Brennan. Gwen."

"The Masquerade is only once a month," Percy supplies. "So you could try to sneak in this weekend, but we won't be there."

Percy's statement seems to disappear amid the charged look Lance is giving me. The blatant offer... the *wish* in his eyes that's so potent I can feel it deep in my core.

I glance at my watch, heartbeat speeding up at the involuntary action spurred by an impulse I shouldn't have. I literally just reprimanded him for flirting.

But I have two hours until I have to be anywhere. My office is in a secluded corner of the second floor, with only an empty staff office next door. This was a distinct drawback, considering what happened, but the dean didn't have an office to move me to in a spot with more foot traffic. The specter of that night still haunts me when I'm in here, though Percy's presence holds it at bay.

But what better way to exorcise that demon than by inviting a more pleasant memory to take its place? To take control in the very place where I lost it six months ago?

"Gwen..." Percy cautions, and I can tell somehow he's caught onto the thoughts racing through my head.

"This is what I need," I say, rising from my chair and looking at him. "You can be involved, if you want. Or you can watch. It's up to you."

Surprisingly he only nods, then looks at Lance. "You need a safe word."

Lance's eyes widen. "I'm not quite sure what's happening here. Why?"

"Because if you want to stop at any point, we need to know."

"How about just *stop*? Not that I'm saying stop *now*. I'm game for whatever she wants. *So* fucking game." He sits up straighter, eyes bright.

"Not good enough," Percy says. "If you don't pick one, I'll pick one for you."

"Fine. Uh… *Friedan*. How's that?"

"I see you've done the reading," I say. "So let's see how you do on your oral presentation."

My heart races, but the eager look he gives me spurs me on. I reach beneath the hem of my skirt and hook my fingers into the sides of my panties, pulling them down and slipping out of them while I hold his gaze. I can feel Percy watching, but he doesn't speak. Either he senses how much I need this, or he's really not as jealous as I thought. Maybe both.

I round my desk and slip into the space before Lance's chair, then prop my backside on the edge of the desk. We're so close my lower legs brush his knees, but he has a death grip on the arms of his chair.

"Is this really happening? I'm not dreaming I'm in a porno or something, am I?"

"Lift my skirt to see for yourself."

He's in khakis and a button-down shirt today, and his arousal is evident from the large bulge in front of his pants. He doesn't immediately follow my order, but glances at Percy as if asking for confirmation that he isn't dreaming.

Percy smirks. "Better do as she asks, sub."

Lance practically whimpers, and his hands shake when he

reaches out to me. He doesn't touch my skirt, but instead slides his hands just beneath the hem, cupping the backs of my thighs. His touch is warm, his caress sending a wave of intense heat all the way to my core. Then he slides his hands up, catching the fabric as he goes and pushing it up to my pelvis.

I'm breathless with anticipation, but he takes his sweet time.

"Jesus," he breathes, gaze tracking his hands as he rubs light caresses over my thighs from the outside in, then pushes them apart. "Touching you is so much better than I imagined."

Then he licks his lips and lowers his head, pressing his mouth to the very top of my bare slit. An involuntary moan slips out with his tongue's first hot slide over my clit. Then the world tilts as he grabs the backs of my thighs, forcing me to lean back as he immerses himself in me like he's been starved for this all week.

I have the forethought to check in with Percy only once, but he isn't watching me. He's too absorbed watching Lance tongue me to oblivion. After a moment, he moves from his spot as sentinel by the door, finally meeting my gaze as he comes around my desk and leans over, mouth at my ear.

"I can't let him have all the fun," he murmurs, cupping the side of my jaw and urging me to turn my head. He captures my mouth with his, and while we kiss, begins to unfasten the buttons of my blouse.

"Percy, if this is too much…" I begin when he releases my mouth for a breath. I'm not sure where I intend to go with my thought because it's hard to maintain the thread of my concern.

"I'll tell you anything you want to know tonight," he says. "For now, let me make you feel good. Lie back."

I feel a soft laugh against my pussy and Lance pulls back. "This is getting fun." His dark eyes flash with amusement and lust as he slides off the chair onto his knees. He drifts both hands down my calves, gently pushing my shoes off, then places a foot on each of his shoulders. "Get comfy, my queen."

He places a kiss against the inside of my knee as I lower myself to the desk, then leans in again, closing his eyes and moaning when he immerses his tongue between my legs once more. The sensation is electrifying and I arch my back, returning the moan when Percy opens my blouse and pushes the top of my bra down, forcing both breasts up and together. He cups them in his hands, rolling my nipples with his thumbs.

I reach up and curl my hand around his neck. "Percy. I'm sorry."

"Hush. Nothing to be sorry for. Just enjoy this."

Then he lowers his mouth to my breast and sucks, and I surrender fully to the two of them.

In the middle of the cloud of pleasure, I become hyperaware of the situation, how little it resembles the horror I felt before. I feel safe with them. Not that I didn't feel safe with Percy, but something about Lance amplifies the sense of being loved and protected, as if the pleasure they give me becomes armor against my trauma.

Tears spring to my eyes and course down the sides of my temples, and my climax arrives quickly. I'm usually chasing that peak, but this time it captures and holds me hostage. For several sublime moments, time stands still. Percy is kissing me to silence my cries, while Lance digs his fingers harder into my thighs. He groans as my pussy spasms violently, my release no doubt drenching him. Sex has never been this good with other men. I enjoyed orgasms in the past, but never like this—never to the point of feeling like every ounce of pleasure was being wrung from my body.

My legs are shaking when Lance finally bestows one final, gentle lick to my clit and pulls back with a sigh. Percy stands over me still, arms braced on either side of me, his gaze intent on mine.

"Better?" he asks.

"Perfect," I breathe, wanting to bask in the moment for as long as possible, but slowly becoming aware of the hard jab of an object under my back. I start to sit, but Percy holds my shoulders.

"One second. Clean her up, will you?" He shoots a look at Lance. I follow his gaze to the dazed and glossy-chinned face, looking even more handsome with the flush in his cheeks.

Lance looks around, frowns, then begins unbuttoning his shirt. He shrugs out of it, wipes his face on one sleeve, then proceeds to gently dry me off. My skirt is still shoved up around my waist, so when I stand, I find it perfectly dry as it falls back down to cover me.

Then I look at Lance and Percy, who's come back around the desk and settled into the chair next to Lance. They're both tense, still sporting hard-ons.

"I didn't intend for this to be all about me. Should we …" I look back at my desk, my papers still right where I left them, as well as the small plastic pencil sharpener that felt so much bigger digging into my spine. My panties are resting on the seat of my chair.

I don't know what I meant to say. Maybe "should we fuck?" but that seems like a terrible idea… more so than what just happened.

"We should get on with our day," Percy says.

"But you're both going to be frustrated. I hate the idea of

leaving you hanging." I look between them, twisting my lips when I glance at each of their crotches.

I'm surprised by Lance's casual shrug. "Hey, I'll survive. I don't want to be like the last asshole who pulled his dick out in this office."

"You could never be like him," I say.

"He's right. We'll survive," Percy says.

"Not sure my *wardrobe* will survive, though." Lance holds up his wrinkled, sodden shirt and looks at Percy. "Any chance you have another spare?"

CHAPTER ELEVEN

PERCY

I wind up leaving Lance and Gwen in her office to get him a fresh shirt from the campus bookstore, but I needed the breather anyway. I've had few to no moments apart from Gwen for months, aside from the few minutes I get at the club when she's around other people we both trust.

It feels strange to be apart, like a tether pulling taut. I don't think she realizes how much I've come to depend on her these last months, how much her need for protection fulfilled my overwhelming need to protect. To reclaim some of the control I've lost in my life after my own trauma. My own failure.

When Chloe approached me about the job, I said no at first. I'd been just a grunt on the security staff for a couple years, refusing promotions despite my resume being more impressive than their current chief of security's, a hawk-eyed former Army Ranger named Amadis. Not that he isn't qualified, but if he knew how far I outranked him when I served, it might make it difficult for him to give me orders.

Chloe's the only one who knows the truth. One of the

requirements of working with her was submitting to a full background check and sharing all the details of my sordid past, but she hasn't given me any reason not to trust her. It took her reminding me of that to get me to agree to the gig as Gwen's full-time bodyguard. She didn't coerce me into it; on the contrary, she pointed out several eerily accurate pain points in my psyche. Things that weren't in my file. Things only a trained psychologist would have understood go deeper than my PTSD.

And she insisted that if I ever wanted to heal, this was the place to start. Sort of like encouraging someone in Alcoholics Anonymous to get a plant, I suppose. Baby steps. She didn't say I had to open up to Gwen, but she also didn't say I ought to *fuck* Gwen. Thanks to that poorly planned moment, we've reached a point where I don't think I have a choice. Part of me wants to, but most of me is fucking terrified of scaring her away.

Now that Lance is apparently in the picture and unlikely to leave unless by force—probably not even then, the way he looks at her—I'll need to step up the intimacy to keep her close. Because I don't know what I'd do if she pulls away, decides she no longer needs a bodyguard, or worst of all, decides she'd rather have someone else watch her back.

Until we figure out who attacked her, I doubt she'll want me gone completely, but I don't want to put any more distance between us than I already have by refusing to open up to her the other night. I didn't lie when I said I'd tell her everything tonight. I just need to find the balls to do it.

I'm still on the fence about trusting Lance, but every instinct tells me he's worth taking a chance on, especially since Saturday night when he trusted me enough to suck him off, and then Tuesday when I found him being beaten by a trio of degenerate trust-fund assholes. The more I learn about the kid, the more I like him, and there's no disputing he's smitten with Gwen.

I have to admit my attraction to him is part of it, but I'd be irresponsible if I let myself get too close. It was getting too close to someone like him that nearly ruined my life before I came back to New York.

I remain lost in my own broody thoughts while I browse through the branded gear section of the bookstore, looking for the most obnoxious T-shirt I can find. It's my duty to keep Lance humble, at the very least. Part of me, however, wants to test him whenever I can. He hesitated when Gwen suggested I suck his dick on Saturday, but obviously enjoyed it once I got busy. I'll convert him to the dark side eventually, but I know it wouldn't be possible if he didn't already have it in him.

Finally I find the shirt I want. It's a white T-shirt with a giant rainbow-striped "PRIDE" emblazoned across the chest, the Columbia lion just beneath it. I grin. I can't wait to see what he thinks of it.

The rear stairwell of the building takes me right to the hallway outside Gwen's office on the second floor. When I push open the door, Dr. MacArthur is standing right outside, head cocked and clearly eavesdropping. He doesn't hear me, so I clear my throat.

"Can I help you?"

He jerks and turns, eyes wide for a second before pasting on an arrogant smile. "Oh, Percy. I thought you were with Ms. Brennan."

"It's *Doctor* Brennan. And she's with a student; I stepped out to run an errand for her. Do you need something?"

Dr. MacArthur is one of the tenured sociology professors in our department. He's an attractive man in his mid-40s with a too-slick look that always gives me hives. I especially can't stand the way he looks at Gwen.

"Of course. My mistake. It isn't important. I just wanted to make sure she received the invitation for the department mixer next month."

"She did, and it's on her calendar. Now if you don't mind." I nod at the door that he's still blocking as if he owns the place. I heard voices from inside when I found him, but they've gone silent now. I hope to fuck the pair weren't discussing anything illicit.

He narrows his eyes, glancing back at the door. "Does Dr. Brennan normally lock her door when she's with a student? That seems highly irregular."

"It depends on the student. When it's one who was recently assaulted by three male classmates, yes. Her office is a safe space for victims." I step closer, squaring my shoulders and daring him to challenge me again. I hope he reads the subtext. As the man in charge of doling out offices to the staff, he's the reason she's stuck in this corner despite what happened, and I'm sure he knows it.

He's only a little shorter, but his ego is about ten times the size of mine, so it takes him a minute to get the hint. Finally he gives me a fake smile and edges past, the faint scent of wintergreen hitting my nose from whatever mint he was sucking on. It does nothing to cover up the undertone of bourbon on his breath.

I wait for him to head back down the hall, but instead he heads for the stairwell door. His office is on the first floor at the other end of the building. Why would he bother coming up here when he could have just called?

My unease over the visit lingers when I knock.

"It's Percy," I say in a low voice. A moment later, the lock clicks and Gwen opens the door to let me in. She steps back to her desk, and I close and lock the door again, then toss the bag from the bookstore to Lance.

"Who were you talking to?" Gwen asks.

"MacArthur. He was lurking right outside when I got back. Eavesdropping. What were you two talking about?"

"The fuck?" Lance's eyebrows draw together. "Does he usually pull shit like that?"

"Not that I know of," Gwen says. "He was probably just coming to nag me about the mixer. I don't even know if I'm going to go."

"That was his excuse, but he was definitely listening in. I have no idea how long he was out there, so I hope your conversation was above-board."

Gwen shakes her head. "We were talking about Lance's class schedule. Did you know he's pre-law? With a 21-credit course load, and on the swim team on top of it."

I'm impressed, but after watching him go down on her twice, it's clear the fucker's an overachiever. I can't ignore the twinge of jealousy when she smiles at him.

"How the fuck did you have time to sneak into the club Saturday night?" I ask.

He smirks and offers a half-shrug. "Hey, I need to blow off steam once in a while too. But she left out the part of the conversation where I shared that my older brother's a cop. I want to see if he can help track down the asshole who assaulted her."

CHAPTER TWELVE

LANCE

*P*ercy stands up straighter, like my announcement just lit a fire under his ass.

"Does he have the resources to help? I got the impression they did all they could, but the lack of any evidence made it difficult."

While he was gone, Gwen confided that he'd offered to get a private detective involved to try to get her some answers, but she turned him down. She just wanted to get on with her life, understandably. What I heard between the lines was that she'd given up, resigned to be swept under the rug of the legal system. Being a minority in this country sucks, and was one of the reasons I chose the major I did.

"He'll do it for me."

"I want to meet him," he says. "Can you make that happen?"

"Sure. Just say where and when." I pull out my phone and look between the two of them, poised to text my brother Ambrose.

"Is he available tonight?" Gwen asks. "We can meet at my house."

"You sure that's a good idea?" Percy asks. The pair lock eyes for a moment, then look at me.

I raise my eyebrows. "I don't have to come. I don't know what's going on here—" I wave between the three of us "—but I'm not about to do anything to jeopardize it."

"There's nothing to jeopardize," Percy says.

He's so emphatic, I laugh. "Seriously? You were there. *Both* times, I might add. And don't tell me this isn't some heavy flirting." I reach into the bag he brought back and pull out the shirt, holding it up. He scowls. I turn it so Gwen can see what the dick pulled *again*.

Gwen covers her face with her hands. "Oh, Percy," she says through a laugh.

I pull the shirt over my head and stand, then close the distance so I'm looking him square in the eyes. My pulse speeds up at the proximity, because I'm about to do something *really* outside my comfort zone to make a point.

He doesn't budge, but stares me down, a muscle spasming in his jaw. In a low voice, I say, "I get it. She's important to you. She's becoming important to me too. But if you think you're going to scare me away with your gay, challenge fucking accepted."

Then I reach up, grab the back of his neck with both hands, and crush my mouth against his before he can react. His surprise is evident from the way he stiffens, but I hold tight, tilting my head to get a deeper lock.

Kissing is something I'm good at, but I've never done it with another man before. But he doesn't resist. Instead he groans and slides one arm around my waist, clamps the other hand at the back of my neck, and closes the minuscule distance between us until our chests are pressed together. Then his tongue darts out and answers my challenge with one of his own, daring me to go deeper. I'm not about to let him win, so I deepen the kiss, our tongues dueling for dominance.

Like a frog in boiling water, I'm not even aware of what's happening to the rest of my body until it's too late, but it's my fault—I jumped into this fucking pot, after all. I even turned on the heat. He tilts his hips, and the hot ridge of his erection grazes mine. Because I'm fucking hard as a rock too. That's when I pull away with a gasp and stare down.

"Holy fuck."

Percy laughs, his fingers still clamped at the back of my neck. "For the record, I'm bi, not gay. And it looks like you might be too." Then he looks at Gwen. "He can come. But only if he agrees to spend the night." Looking back at me, he adds, "Because you started something, and I'll be damned if I don't make you finish it."

When I pull away with a chuckle, I'm about to suggest we slow down, but Gwen's shocked expression makes me hold my tongue. She's staring at Percy like he's insane. Did she really not know his orientation? She was the one who asked him to suck my dick.

"How…?" she asks, glancing at the tent in his trousers.

He grimaces. "You have to admit, he is kind of lovable. I'm not a machine."

Confused about the exchange, I clear my throat. "It's totally true, but I don't get why you're surprised."

"She's surprised because it takes a lot to make me hard. Don't let it go to your fucking head, okay?"

"That's an oversimplification," Gwen says, but clamps her mouth shut at Percy's warning glare. She smiles. "Fine, you can deny all you want, but you can't hide the truth from me."

"Fuck, you guys are talking in riddles now. I have to go. I have a cubicle at the library reserved to work on my thesis. I need to get going if I'm going to be stuck with the two of you all night."

I stuff my soiled shirt into my backpack, then remember my abandoned text to my brother. I add the meeting details and hit send, then press Gwen and Percy for their numbers.

The tension of my undertaking weighs on me all the way to the library. It's unlike me to get this distracted from my academic obligations, but I've always been good at multitasking and compartmentalizing. Except now it's a bigger challenge than usual, because my mind is still spinning about the revelation Percy laid on me.

I *did* initiate that kiss, but it was more a challenge to his need to fuck with me. I knew I was right, but I didn't have to fucking *kiss him* to prove it. So what does that say about me?

At least Gwen has some good memories of sexy-time in her office now. I think I'd have done even more with Percy, if she needed it to purge the demons from that small space.

I struggle to shift focus to my thesis research, because I keep thinking about the moment she dropped her panties. I'm pent-up as hell but there's no outlet for me now. I'm not going back to my room to jerk off, and I'm not idiotic enough to try to do it in the library, no matter how isolated it is in the little cubby I usually choose for working in the stacks. I was amazed at how much self-restraint Percy manages around her, but now that I know he has trouble getting a hard-on, I kind of envy him.

But I guess I do it for him, because there was no mistaking his erection when we were pressed together—nor mine.

I groan, shake my head violently to dispel the spiraling thoughts, and redouble my efforts to focus. It takes serious work, but eventually the dry material of my research notes kills my libido, and I'm actually able to read ten words without thinking of either of them again for the next few hours.

When I leave the library, I stop by the cafeteria for some cheap institutional pizza I shove into my face while I bike to the address Gwen gave me. Her place is a quaint brownstone not far from the college, a block away from fraternity row. Ambrose is already there, waiting on the step. He's off his shift, but still in his uniform. He gives me a quizzical look when I hop off my bike and secure it to the iron rail at the bottom of the steps.

"What's with this getup?" he asks. "And what the fuck happened to your face?"

"Huh?" I give him a blank look.

"You need to tell me something, *hermano*?" He stares pointedly at my chest, then gestures to my two black eyes.

I glance down at my shirt, realizing I'm still in the rainbow Pride shirt Percy bought for me.

"Ah... it's complicated." I debate coming clean with him here and now, but hesitate. I'm still not quite sure what's going on.

He crosses his arms. "Sum up. I have all night, and I'm sure your friends can wait."

My nostrils flare. He's a stubborn bastard, and I know he'll stand firm until he gets what he wants.

I squint apprehensively and scrub a hand over the top of my head. "Um, they might be more than friends? Like I said, it's complicated."

"I thought you said I'm meeting your teacher."

Clearing my throat, I nod. "Uh, yeah. And her TA. Can we just go in? Please keep an open mind. She needs your help."

"Lead the way," he says with a shake of his head.

I hit the doorbell, stomach doing acrobatics. While we

wait, Ambrose leans in a little from beside me and gives a loud sniff.

"What the fuck?" I stage whisper. My eyes widen and I lean away. Then it hits me that I may have a clean shirt, but I haven't showered since my encounter with Gwen's epic pussy earlier.

Ambrose just shakes his head and utters a curse in Spanish. He plasters on a smile when the door cracks open and Percy appears.

At least my brother is on his best behavior for the visit, and thank fuck he doesn't talk shit about me the way I dreaded he might. Ambrose can be an enormous dick, but I guess he knows how to behave in mixed company.

He's serious when he sits down with Gwen at her dining table and starts going over the case. I'm too distracted being in her house to pay close attention, but Percy's perched on a barstool at the kitchen island nearby, watching like a hawk. When Percy explains finding me getting beaten to shit over something another student said about Gwen, Ambrose gives me an appraising look.

I'm too antsy to sit, so I wander into the home office near the front door, which is decorated in a way that suits Gwen perfectly, with neutral-toned furniture and carpet, walls trimmed in white molding, and splashes of color coming from the striking artwork mounted in aesthetically pleasing spots. There's another prismatic array stemming from the rainbow of books occupying the built-in shelves lining two sides of the room.

I peek closer and find volume upon volume of romance novels. Scanning the spines, I pick out a title I actually recognize. It's the book about the club that helped me track down its location Saturday night. But there's not just one—it's a series so long it fills an entire shelf.

I pull out the first one and peek inside, eyes widening at my discovery. It has a glossary of terms in the front, but it's the story itself I become engrossed with, barely aware of finding a comfy armchair in the corner and sitting down to keep reading.

"There you are," Gwen says. I jerk my head up and close the book abruptly, shoving it between my knees. My cheeks heat.

"Uh, hi. I was just, um…" *I was just reading porn, but don't mind me.*

She quirks a smile at me. "Your brother's about to go. I think he has enough information."

"Hot!" I stand and set the book back onto the chair, giving my brother an interested look where he stands in the doorway to the room. "You can help, right?"

"I can call in a couple favors. Get some security footage of the building and see what's up. Nine times out of ten, it's an acquaintance or colleague in cases like this, so keep an eye out, because he's probably someone you see regularly."

"No shit," I say, frowning. Who the hell would do something like that? My mind turns to the shitbirds from class. I'm going to be on those assholes like glue from now on, I don't care what they do to me.

Gwen opens the door. "Thanks so much for your help, Officer Lacosta."

"My pleasure, Dr. Brennan. Hope we can find the perpetrator for you, give you some peace of mind."

"I'll walk you out," I say.

The door closes behind us, and we step out into the warmth of a late spring evening. On the walk to his car, Ambrose says, "Nice woman. I get the sense that Percy isn't just her TA, though. Too much overprotective alpha-tude from him."

"He's her bodyguard."

Ambrose nods. "Figured as much. So where do you fit in?"

"Just a concerned student." There's no way in hell I'm telling my brother what happened on Saturday. Where I found the two of them. Their extracurricular hobbies have no bearing on the investigation anyway.

He shoots me a suspicious look. "You know I know you're full of shit. You smell like you showered in *coño,* and those bruises are like neon signs this goes deeper. I know you too well to believe the two are unrelated. Was he the one who gave you that shiner?"

I touch the healing bruise under one eye. "No, he actually saved me when I got into it with a couple other students from her class—rich dicks talking shit about her. That's all."

Ambrose nods, his lips pressed tight together. "Just be careful. This goes bad for you, I'll be the one picking up the pieces."

I silently stare into the distance. I know he's thinking about how much ass-kicking he had to do just to get me to graduate from high school. We've been each other's only family since our dad left when we were kids. It's through luck alone that I didn't wind up in foster care, but Ambrose came through for me then, and I've vowed ever since not to disappoint him.

"You know I won't do anything to fuck up my scholarship," I say when we reach his black and white.

He just eyes me and shakes his head. "The age difference isn't lost on me. My gut says you're trying to fill a void with this older woman. You've done it before, just not to this extent."

"This isn't some Oedipal complex, I promise. And it wasn't with my shrink, either." Though I can't deny I formed a particularly strong attachment to the therapist Ambrose started taking me to when I began acting out in a big way in junior high. I hadn't had a mom in five years, and it took a toll.

But Gwen's nothing like Dr. Mathis, and she definitely doesn't resemble any of my memories of Mom that haven't faded after all these years since she was killed.

I clench my teeth, pinning my brother with a stare that warns him not to dig deeper. He knows I don't like discussing this topic. We restrict conversations about Mom to one day a year, and that's it. Today is not that day.

He shakes his head. "Well, don't do anything stupid. Let me do my job. Need a ride back to campus? I'm headed that way."

"I'm actually staying."

He laughs. "Now why am I not surprised?"

CHAPTER THIRTEEN

GWEN

"What's on your mind?" Percy asks after sitting for several minutes at my kitchen island without a word. I've been staring into the tea I made, to try calming my anxiety after sharing the details of my attack with Lance's brother.

"It still leaves me feeling raw every time I have to tell someone," I confess.

"Well, hopefully that's the last time you'll have to. Tell me what you need."

I glance at the front door. "I need him to come back. You did say he had to spend the night, right?"

"He'll be back. But Gwen, you know I can do everything he can do, right? That's why I'm here."

Taking a deep breath, I look at Percy over the island and our steaming mugs. "You're here to help me feel safe. You're here because I can trust you with anything. But I want you to trust me too. What I want from you now requires more trust than I think you've granted me so far."

He stares down at the marble top between us, swallows, and sighs. "Yes. And I promised I'd tell you tonight. I'm waiting for him to get back, because if he's going to be a fixture with you, I don't want to have to tell this story more than once. I hope you understand."

His expression is beseeching, and the weight of the request hits home. There's a deeper reason Chloe chose him to be my bodyguard, but his deflection makes it clear he isn't ready to share.

"What makes you think he's going to be a fixture?"

Percy chuckles. "Don't you think I know you well enough by now to recognize when you're letting someone in? You barely trust anyone who isn't connected to the club. He shouldn't have even been there, but he was. He rocked your world once, and now all of a sudden you're letting him go down on you in your office. Not at the club, but where you work."

My nostrils flare at the dismissive way he characterizes our encounter this afternoon. "It isn't just *where I work*, and you know that. That office was where I lost control of my life. I've been struggling to claw it back ever since. Why can't you just admit you're jealous of him?"

His shoulders drop and he shakes his head. "Because I'm not jealous. What I feel is way too complicated to be reduced to that. For a start, I wouldn't have sucked his dick if I didn't want to. I'm not suggesting I don't want him here with us, Gwen; I'm saying the opposite, even though it's fucking crazy to let myself want it. I mean, he's a decade younger than both of us, for one thing."

That leaves my next retort withering on my tongue. I stare at him for a beat, then say, "You want him here?" My eyes narrow. "Did you know who he was at the club, or did you just figure it out on Tuesday?"

"I didn't know at first. Something was familiar about him,

but I just figured I knew him from the club. He reminded me of Jude and Simon a little. Remember them?"

That provokes a smile from me. "Yes, and I'm still working up the nerve to try out their machine."

"Let's work up to that," he says. He's smiling now, and some of the tension that built up during our conversation eases, but it doesn't completely subside.

I glance toward the front room when I hear the door open and close. Three solid clicks follow—the sound of my three deadbolts being engaged. I can't help but feel a little warmer.

"Good for him," Percy murmurs.

When Lance appears in the arch of my kitchen doorway, I push a third steaming mug across the island toward him. "I made you tea."

His eyebrows lift, and he smiles as he steps in and settles on the barstool next to me. "I'm not much of a tea drinker, but this kicks ass. Thank you."

After a moment of both Percy and me watching him take a few sips, he sets his mug down and looks at us both. "What did I miss?"

Percy takes a breath, bracing his fists on the counter.

I intercept the question. "We were just discussing how you fit in, because I'd like to keep you."

He squares his shoulders, and I can tell he's barely containing his excitement. "Oh yeah? That's fantastic. I am happy to be kept." He grins at me, but then his expression turns serious as he looks at Percy. "You're good with this, yeah?"

"I am," Percy says, his voice pitched low enough to make warmth pool deep within me. When Lance smirks, Percy adds, "Don't let it go to your head, kid. We both answer to her."

Lance nods and clears his throat, fidgeting with the tab of the teabag hanging over the rim of his mug. "So about that... I'm clueless as to how the whole submissive thing works. Do I just do whatever you tell me all the time? Like... does it extend to things like '*do your homework*' and shit like that?"

I sit up straighter, because it hasn't really hit me until now that I need to decide what the dynamic will be between us. Looking at Percy for guidance, I'm met with an arched eyebrow and a smirk, as if to say, *You started this, you finish it.*

Realizing I'm getting no help from him, I take a breath and face Lance. "It can, but only if that's what you need. It can be about dominance entirely, or only partially." I trail off when I see him frown. "What's wrong?"

"I didn't think what I needed was part of the equation. This is about you not feeling powerless after what happened to you."

That makes me pause and regroup, because I'm not prepared for his show of empathy. He's surprised me at every turn, to the point I'd almost rather spend more time talking to him. But I've already started down this path and want to make sure I do it right.

"Your needs are absolutely important, Lance. If submission isn't something you enjoy, tell me. In fact, if there's *anything* we do that you don't like, you need to communicate that. This relationship won't work if we're not one hundred percent honest with each other."

"Is there something you wanted to say?" Percy asks.

Lance shrugs. "Only that I don't think I can stand it if I have to go all day without an— um—*outlet*, after what happened earlier. But I'm here for you, so I didn't want to center my dick in the conversation, you know?"

Percy laughs, and I shoot him a look, because what Lance said was unbearably sweet.

"I'm sorry. You're just nothing like I expected. Seriously, you give new meaning to the term kiss-ass," Percy says when he catches his breath.

Lance scowls. "I'm not saying it to be an ass-kisser. She told me what happened to her. I imagine dicks are the last thing she wants to have to manage after that. So that's why everything has to be about her taking pleasure from us, not the other way around."

"Oh, Lance." I stand and cup both his cheeks, looking into his eyes. "You are so precious, but I don't have a phobia of dicks. My only hard limit right now is blowjobs, but I'm hoping that won't last forever. That doesn't mean I want you to leave a scene frustrated. This afternoon was spontaneous, but from now on, I promise you'll get some form of outlet."

"I wasn't complaining," he says, his gaze falling to my mouth and lingering there. "Do with me what you will. If it means I have to jerk off more, so be it. I just didn't have time this afternoon."

I silence him with a kiss, which he returns with fervor, but I can feel the tension of restraint coiled through his body. I'm tempted to tell him he can touch me, but I don't want to waste his absolute willingness to follow my lead.

"Come with me," I say, gripping him by the hand and leading him toward the rear stairs. I glance back at Percy.

"I'll clean up and be right behind you," he says, gathering the mugs from the counter as I continue up the narrow staircase at the rear of my kitchen.

"So, are there rules?" Lance asks.

"The only real rule is to communicate. Other than that, since this is new, we can figure it out as we go. You should know that this is new to me too."

"Seriously? You were so... *perfect* Saturday night. You looked like you'd been doing it for ages."

"My experience with dominance is pretty much limited to my throne at Whitewood. That night with you was the first time I did anything remotely different than just choosing a subject to pleasure me. It was the first time Percy participated more actively too. We both learned a lot about ourselves and each other, thanks to you."

"Well, it was hot as fuck. So I'm game to be your guinea pig if you want to try anything else."

We reach my bedroom and I aim for the blue velvet fainting couch I have situated in a small sitting area between my mirrored closet door and my bed.

"What did you like best?" I ask when I urge him to sit.

His gaze drifts to the ceiling as he ponders the question, a flush rising to his cheeks. The front of his jeans moves, betraying his arousal at whatever's going through his mind. Finally he smiles and says, "Being shackled to your chair. Forced to do your bidding. To be used by you and Percy. I never realized how hot it could be to let another guy suck me off."

"You're attracted to him. This is new to you, isn't it?"

He coughs into his hand, holding his fist up to conceal a smile. "Surprised the fuck out of me, but yeah." Then he frowns. "Should I return the favor, do you think?"

"I think that's up to Percy. If you want to experiment more with him, we can make it happen."

"You mean like, ordering me to do things with him?"

I raise my eyebrows at his eager tone, because I hadn't even hinted at anything like that, but it's clearly something he's thought about.

"Sure, if you're both willing participants. But I think he'd be game."

"Game for what?" Percy steps into the bedroom and closes the door behind him.

"You'll see," I say with a sly look. I stand and move to the end of the bed, facing them. "Take off your clothes, both of you."

"Oh, we're diving right in then, I see," Percy says with a tinge of amusement. He glances at Lance. "Any hints about what she has in mind?"

Lance rises and strips off his rainbow T-shirt, then moves to stand facing me beside Percy. "Just some good, dirty fun."

The pair move in unison, unzipping and shoving their pants down their legs. My stomach turns a flip at how utterly beautiful both men are, and that they're both willing to do everything I ask. The problem is I have so many ideas, I'm not sure where to start.

Lance darts a surreptitious glance at Percy, his gaze slipping down to Percy's groin. "How the fuck are you not hard as steel right now?"

"Because I'm not a horny twenty-one-year-old," Percy retorts.

"It's a fair question," I say. "I think I can remedy the issue, though."

I close the distance to Percy, slipping close enough that our chests touch. I look up into his eyes, gauging his mood. We haven't finished our conversation yet, and the look in his eyes says he's aware of this, but I want to give him a reprieve for now. I at least trust him enough to know he'll follow through on his promise.

I clasp his chin and raise my mouth to his. He presses a kiss against my lips, tentatively darting his tongue out to touch mine. The same rush of sensation floods through me at the feel of him. I hold on, teasing back with my tongue as I slide my other hand down between his legs, drifting my knuckles along the side of his flaccid cock, then cupping his balls. He groans into our kiss, and his cock rouses as I fondle him.

"That's better," I say after a moment. I step back and observe the pair. Both their bodies are wound tighter, their cocks erect and engorged. "Now face each other and wait for me."

CHAPTER FOURTEEN

PERCY

Gwen steps into her walk-in closet, turns on the light, and closes the door. I narrow my eyes at the smirk I catch before she disappears, but there's nothing to do but obey her command.

Lance heaves a shaky breath and turns when I do.

"So, how does this go? Any clues on what I can expect?"

"Your guess is as good as mine," I say. "Just remember to use your safe word if it gets to be too much."

"I don't know, man. I kind of want *too much* if she's the one delivering. I want it all."

I study him for a breath. "Even me? Because it isn't lost on me that being intimate with another man is new to you, and I have a sense that's where this is going."

His Adam's apple bobs with a rough swallow, and he nods. "I want to try. I just hope I can hold out, because I'm really fucking horny. Like, uncomfortably horny."

The closet door clicks open and we both turn. We're greeted with a sight that makes Lance utter a curse. I'm just as surprised, because seeing Gwen in full-on dominatrix gear was the last thing I expected. I didn't even know she owned anything like this.

She's in a black satin corset with red pinstripes that doesn't cover her breasts at all, but pushes their full roundness up and forward. Black garters adorn the tops of her thighs, attached to stockings that disappear into thigh-high leather stiletto boots. Her hands are covered in matching black satin gloves that extend halfway up her biceps. She isn't wearing panties, and her bare snatch glistens at the very center.

"Good boys," she croons as she strides toward us. We're both transfixed, and I think Lance has stopped breathing. I might have also.

When she reaches us, she rests a hand on each of our shoulders, slides down to our wrists, and lifts our hands, placing them on her breasts. Despite her poise, a deep flush warms her dark complexion, and she tilts her head back a little, looking into my eyes, then Lance's as she guides both our hands over her breasts, teasing herself with our fingertips before sliding us lower.

"Jesus," Lance whispers when she pulls our hands over her hips, then lets go.

"Feel me, both of you," she breathes.

I continue the path she began, dipping my hand lower, past the edge of her corset to her warm, smooth skin.

"Do you mean…" Lance begins, then says, "Never mind," when he sees me coast my fingers between her thighs. He follows, attention rapt when his fingers join mine.

She's soaked, her wetness coating my fingertips when I glide them between her slick lips, careful to stay to one side. Lance takes the other, his breathing quickening.

"Jesus, you're so wet," he murmurs.

His knuckles brush mine when we delve farther between

her thighs.

"You can have this all to yourself, if you do what I ask," she says. She grips his wrist again, and I remove my hand as she urges his farther between her legs. "Do you want to fuck me, Lance?"

The poor guy lets out a desperate groan that might have been, "Fuck yes." I totally empathize.

Gwen suddenly steps back, leaving him standing with outstretched hand, fingers coated in her juices.

"Then you need to make Percy come while I watch. When you succeed, this pussy is all yours."

"Devious," I say.

"Don't waste time, sweetie," she says, planting her feet wide and crossing her arms. She's a wet dream with her tits framed the way they are and her bare pussy shining with her juices. It takes a moment for me to register that Lance is frozen in place, obviously still processing her command.

"You know how dicks work," I say. "Mine's no different than yours."

"I—I know. Is that what you want? For me to suck you off?"

I lift an eyebrow. "Handjobs are on the table, but not nearly as fun, and I'm betting you're not ready to let me fuck you."

His mouth drops open, so I take matters into my own hands—or rather, into *his*. I grab the hand he just had between Gwen's legs, then step in, closing the distance between us as I cup the back of his head.

"It's not as difficult as you think," I say, then kiss him. I wrap his hand around my dick while we kiss, banking on him getting the hint once he's got me.

He figures it out, squeezing his fingers around my dick and giving me a gentle tug. Pleasure blasts through me so hard my head spins. I release his mouth to let out a rough groan when he strokes the full length of my dick, thumb rubbing along the underside until he reaches my tip. He pauses and smiles when the pad of his thumb finds the pre-cum coating my tip and rubs in a circle.

I'm too preoccupied with the way his big hand feels on me to pay much attention to Gwen, but I'm vaguely aware that she's moved to the end of her bed and settled on it, legs primly crossed like she isn't half-naked.

Then he drops to his knees, and my eyes widen. I suppose I truly thought he'd settle for giving a handjob.

"What?" he asks, peering up at me with a grin. "She wants a show, so we ought to give it to her."

I'd kiss the fucker if he wasn't about to suck my dick. I'm about to respond, but lose track of every thought when he grips the base of my cock and slides his lips over my tip.

He's hesitant at first, tentatively sliding his tongue around in a way that makes an involuntary groan rise from deep inside me. My hips tilt toward him as he takes me deeper. His brows furrow with concentration and he grips me tighter, swallowing me even farther.

"Jesus," I blurt when he manages to take me all the way to my fucking root. Fuck me, does this guy even have a gag reflex? His throat flexes, and I can feel the spasm against the tip of my cock, every warm, wet contour of his mouth and tongue teasing me to distraction. Then he slides back off and looks up at me. The hand that still grips my cock begins to stroke.

"What do you like?" he asks. "Just that? Humming? Ball fondling? Ass play?"

I can only blink dumbly through the pleasure. "Yes," is all I manage.

He chuckles. "Then here we go."

Those lips wrap around me again and I lose myself, because he seems determined to do all the things. He takes me deep again and starts to suck, pistoning his mouth up and down my dick with perfect rhythm and just the right level of friction from his lips and tongue.

Then he begins to hum, a low, deep rumble from his chest that buzzes all the way up my length. He pauses only once, long enough to stick two fingers into his mouth and wet them before sucking me deep again.

My ass tingles in anticipation, and I'm not disappointed when he cups my balls, sliding those two fingers behind them, probing across my perineum to press against my opening. I relax and let out a curse when his fingers penetrate me.

In the midst of it, Gwen lets out a soft sigh, and I look over. I'm graced by the sight of her propped on one arm with her legs spread, her fingers stroking her wet, pink pussy. Her head is tilted, and she's watching Lance pleasure me while she pleasures herself.

The view is galvanizing and reminds me why he's being an overachiever at trying to get me off. I decide to give him a taste of what it's like to be on his knees for a man. I grip his head, tangling my fingers into his hair, and start thrusting. He stiffens at first, then relaxes, meeting my rhythm with the bob of his head. His fingers slide deeper and hit me in just the right spot, which makes my dick twitch and spasm.

"Holy fucking Christ," I mutter when he begins finger-fucking my ass faster. Pleasure rushes to all my extremities and my vision blurs. My orgasm builds fast, almost too fast, but I manage to blurt out, "Here it comes. Fuck!"

I half-expect him to pull back, but he just takes me all the way down his throat one last time, shoves his fingers in me to the last knuckles, and hooks them, and I let loose, shooting every ounce of my orgasm right down his throat.

CHAPTER FIFTEEN

LANCE

I'm buzzed from lack of breath as much as the gratification of the new experience. I'm a bit of a competitive dick over just about everything, so why should sucking dick be any different?

"You're good, man. Go get your prize," Percy says, tapping me on the shoulder. He's still hard, even though he dumped what felt like a gallon of semen down my throat.

I slide my mouth off him and swallow again, still absorbing the new experience. The flavor wasn't what I expected—I've tasted my own cum, but it tasted nothing like his. His was *sweet*, which I was totally unprepared for. I make a mental note to ask him how he manages that, then stand and face the bed.

Gwen is bright-eyed, biting her lower lip and leaning back on both arms, her perfect tits poised and just asking to be sucked on. I'm so turned on my whole body hurts with the need, but I just want to take her in for a moment.

She's been busy, from the looks of it. Her knees are wide, her pussy spread and glistening, and she has one hand resting on her mound, fingers wet from stroking herself.

I have the urge to drop to my knees and use my mouth on her again when I remember that I get to have more this time.

"Come fuck me now. You earned it," she says.

"Do I get to choose how I fuck you?" I ask. Because I've scoped out her room, and I have ten million fantasies of fucking her in here already stored away in my brain, but if I can only live one of them, I know which one it is.

"Of course."

I reach for her hand and help her stand, then lead her to the blue sofa, turn her away from me, and press myself to her back. "Bend over," I whisper in her ear.

She climbs onto the sofa, kneeling as she grips the back of it. I turn to look in the mirror on her closet door, enjoying the perfect view of her reflected profile and my naked body behind her.

Gwen cocks her head and laughs. "Why am I not surprised you want to see everything?"

"You're good with this?" I ask, closing the distance and resting my hands on her round, full ass. I slide my hands up her back to her shoulders and down again, coasting the fingers of both hands down her crack to spread her pussy. My gaze tracks every touch, alert to her responses. She lets out a breathy moan when I graze her clit.

"Good with what, exactly? I already said you can fuck me. I want you to."

"Without a condom, I mean."

"I think we settled that when you sent your blood test to me. We're all quite safe."

"Thank fuck," I murmur. "Because I'm going to fill you so full of my cum, it'll be dripping out of you in class next week."

I slot my tip between the luscious swell of her labia, rubbing up and down just to feel her heat and wetness. She's fucking heaven and I'm not even inside her yet. I'm going to blow my load so fast, but need to rein things in, because I'll be damned if I come before her.

But when I press into her, her moan is so strong a catalyst I know I'm not going to last, and there's not a damn thing I can do about it. I bottom out and freeze, holding her hips in a death grip while I take several deep breaths and try to reclaim some control.

Her muscles tighten around me, and I let out a strangled groan. "Don't. Fucking. Move. Or I'm going to come."

She looks over her shoulder. "Yes. And you'll keep fucking me until you come again. And again. You're not allowed to stop until your balls are dry, Lance."

That elicits a whimper, because she's tapped into a very particular dirty fantasy of mine. I'm not even sure I'm capable of doing what she says, but I'm going to try.

It takes merely two strokes for me to lose it. My cock spasms, and I shoot into her with a groan. I fold myself over her back, cock still pulsing into her depths.

"Sorry," I say against her cheek. "It's been a long day."

She reaches back and combs her fingers into my hair, craning her head around to kiss me.

"Did I say you could stop moving?" she says when she pulls back and meets my fevered gaze.

I chuckle. "I guess not." I begin to move, glad my dick didn't soften inside her, but not really surprised.

She sighs and pushes back, meeting my rhythm. It's easier this time, and I'm so over-sensitized that every stroke feels as good as if I just started fucking her. But the pleasure builds more slowly at least, and her own slippery juices mix with mine for the perfect balance that feels so goddamn good I find a second wind.

"Harder," she says.

I comply, holding tighter to her hips and jacking into her as fast and hard as I can. I glance to the mirror and stare, watching in fascination as we fuck. She's beautiful all bent over like that. The view is obscured for a moment when Percy crosses before the mirror and moves to settle on the sofa beside her.

"What do you need?" he asks, and I realize he's directing the question to me and not Gwen.

Another orgasm is a little beyond my reach right now, but I'm determined to fulfill my promise. Twice isn't enough; I want to see my cum dripping out of her pussy when I'm finished.

"Stick your fingers in my ass," I say.

Percy smiles. "I can do you one better. Do you trust me?"

The gleam in his eyes makes me slow.

"Oh god, don't fucking stop!" Gwen demands.

"Yeah, I trust you," I say, breathless from exertion. I don't really care what he does. I want it all.

He disappears again, and then I feel him slide up behind me. He presses against my back. He's not hard anymore, but my ass clenches anyway. I did just ask him to violate me, and despite how hot the idea sounds, I'm a complete anal virgin.

I lose rhythm for a moment, hyperfocused on the sensation of his chest against my back and his mouth on my neck. He bites down on the fleshy part of my shoulder while his hands squeeze my hips, then slide between us to grip my ass. He spreads my cheeks, grinding against me, his dick half-hard again—just enough to tease pressure against my anus, but not come close to penetrating. The pressure is intense, though, and nearly makes me come, but he pulls back and kneels.

He spreads my ass wider, and the next thing I feel is his tongue. It's a hot, wet, slick, and so, so erotic sensation.

"Fuck, fuck, fuck! I can't…" My words are constricted by a strangled groan as my dick erupts for the second time inside Gwen's pussy. My vision blurs, but I hold on tight, letting the whole surreal experience envelop me. I'm floating on a cloud of pleasure with Percy's tongue still stroking my tight hole, barely even penetrating, but it's enough to keep my dick spasming for several seconds.

He eases back, and I take a breath. My eyesight clears, and I stare down at Gwen's ass. She looks over her shoulder at me, lower lip gripped between her teeth, her expression telling me she's desperate to come. I'm expecting her to tell me she's had enough and it's her turn now, but she surprises me.

"Do it again," she commands. "I want you to come inside me until you can't anymore."

I blink rapidly and chuckle. "You're a goddamn demon, woman."

But I'm not about to disobey the queen. I pull out, my dick flagging, but the sight of creamy fluid coating her wetness sends a fresh current of want through my body. I have the physical stamina for this; I just don't know if I have the *sexual* stamina. But I'm damn sure going to give it my best shot.

"Need more help?" Percy asks. He's still on his knees behind me, but isn't touching me. He reaches up and grips one ass cheek again, this time grazing his thumb between and pressing into the slickness left by his tongue.

I clench involuntarily, then relax, absorbing the pleasant sensation that increases to an electrifying friction as he pushes deeper into me. And wouldn't you know it, my dick gets hard again.

"Fuck, you know all the right buttons to push, don't you?" I begin to fuck Gwen slowly, taking a more leisurely pace.

This time I release her hips and just undulate mine, staring down at the milky slickness that coats us both.

After a moment, I catch her watching me, a slight smile on her gorgeous face.

"Look at yourself," she says, tilting her chin to the mirror. "You're magnificent."

I turn my head to view our reflection, mesmerized by the play of light over my muscles, on the fevered look in Gwen's eyes and the arch of her back each time she pushes against my thrusts. Behind me, Percy watches too, then leans in and clamps his teeth onto the flesh of one ass cheek while at the same time pushing his thumb deeper.

I close my eyes at the flood of pure pleasure when the pad of his thumb presses against some deep part of me, the contact blasting even more ecstasy through my every vein. Out of the blue, I wonder what it would feel like to let him fuck me.

I open my eyes and meet his gaze in the mirror, licking my lips at the strangeness of this new desire. He's hard too. I swallow, trying to generate saliva to wet my suddenly dry mouth, and the remnants of his cum wash over my tongue.

"I want you to fuck me," I blurt.

His eyebrows shoot up. At the same time, Gwen lets out a surprised laugh.

Percy shakes his head. "I'm game, but let's take things one step at a time." He stares at me in the mirror and twists his thumb in my ass. "You'll need more prep than this, for one thing, unless you've got a secret you want to share. For tonight, we're doing what *she* wants, though."

An involuntary breath eases out of me. Relief? Surrender? I'm not sure, but I nod and look at Gwen again. She's studying me intently in the mirror.

"Can you come for me one more time?"

"If he keeps doing that, I'm damn sure going to come."

His touch is gentle, but still the stretch of his thumb, and the friction of his knuckle is a little painful, but the slight pain is overridden by the pleasure. I want more, but I'm also a little scared of it, so I'm glad he said no.

"Percy," Gwen says. "There's a bottle of lube in the nightstand. Why don't you get it and give Lance a little more of what he wants? And Lance, when he gets it, I want you to do the same to me. Stretch my ass with your fingers while you fuck me."

I can't help but look at her tight, puckered opening, spread wide and glistening from the mess I've made of her so far. Experimentally I graze my thumb over her hole, and she lets out a gratifying moan.

Then Percy appears with a tube in his hand and squeezes it over her crack. Clear, viscous fluid drizzles out, coating her. I rub it around, entranced by the way she clenches and releases, each flex tightening all her muscles around my dick too.

I push my thumb against her opening and feel it give, then push into her all the way to my knuckle. She tightens again and I start fucking her harder, pistoning my thumb in and out of her with the same rhythm as my dick plunging in and out of her pussy.

When Percy kneels behind me again, I'm so ready. I widen my stance, eager for what he's about to do. First he cups my balls, his hand coated with the lube. He strokes them for several seconds, working the lube around and up my perineum, the slickness an entirely new sensation. It feels fucking amazing.

Then he breaches me with his thumb again, and it's even better than before.

"Relax," he croons. "Bear down a little and I can fill you up even more."

As if demonstrating what I need to do, Gwen's tight anus relaxes around my thumb. I get the hint and shift my hand, this time pushing two fingers into her. A moment later, I feel a thicker penetration in my own ass. My cock spasms, but I keep fucking, my endurance higher now after having come twice already.

Just like before, it takes only a few pumps of Percy's fingers in my ass before I'm losing track of reality. I'm nothing but a bundle of pure, raw sensation when my climax takes me and I shoot another load into her. I'm sure I'm spent, but Percy's fingers dig deeper, pressing and massaging that spot again.

"Ah, fuck!" I yell. My orgasm stretches into infinity, and I bend over Gwen's back, holding on and clutching her breasts. The shift in position only gives Percy more access, and he starts massaging my balls with a slick hand again, his breath hot against my tailbone.

"I'm so glad you asked me to fuck you, Lance. I'm going to hold you to it, and it's going to be fucking spectacular when I do."

CHAPTER SIXTEEN

GWEN

*L*ance is moaning, and maybe even drooling a little against my neck, when his orgasm finally eases and Percy releases him. He remains inside me and I clench around him a few times, enjoying the soft grunts he lets out when my muscles tighten on his dick.

He moves slightly, pulling back and thrusting in again. My body is still alight with need for more, but I wanted to reward him for waiting so long after making me come earlier today.

"Want to make you happy," he murmurs. The sentiment warms my heart. Even though I know he probably just means he wants to make me come, I love the thought that he might mean more.

"I am happy," I say. "You can relax and take a breather if you want. I'm not close to done with you yet, honey."

I reach back and curl my fingers through his thick, dark hair, then crane my head so I can meet his mouth with mine. He hums into the kiss, drawing it out in a lingering, delicious tangle of our tongues. When I release him, I catch sight of

Percy reclining on the floor beside us, elbow propped on the sofa. He's alert, eyes bright and hungry.

"Give him a turn," I say, tapping Lance on the hip. He heaves a breath and draws himself back. The effort it takes to disengage is almost comical, his eyes filled with wonder and want when he stares down at my drenched pussy.

"Holy fuck. If I had it in me, I wouldn't stop fucking you. Ever. But I guess it's only fair to share, right? She's all yours, *hermano*."

I meet Percy's gaze when Lance moves back. "How do you want me?" I ask.

"You're the queen," he says in a low voice. "But I think you might want a change of scenery."

"What did you have in mind?"

"Stand up," he says.

When I do, he rises to sit on the sofa and slides to the center where my knees were a moment ago. "Facing me or him?" he asks.

I ponder the possibilities for a moment before turning my back to Percy and straddling his legs. Bending forward slightly, I reach between my legs to grip his cock and stroke, then align him with my pussy. I'm still aching from all the stimuli without any release, and his cock feels like heaven when it fills me. The truth is both of them have a similar curve to their cocks that means this position feels better. And I doubt it makes much difference to either of them.

But the real reason—one I think my subconscious knew but isn't apparent to me at first—becomes clear when I settle with Percy's cock deep in me.

He wraps his strong arms around my torso and pulls me back against his strong chest, then nuzzles my neck.

"Hmm, I like this," he says as he begins tilting his hips up with languid thrusts. His embrace overwhelms me with sensations of protection, safety, and intense pleasure. I surrender to his hold, reaching back to grip the top of the sofa for leverage to move my hips to meet his thrusts.

Lance is seated on the bed, his body glistening with sweat and his cock still coated with us both. He watches raptly, looking like he's trying desperately to summon the energy to join in. After several seconds of staring, his gaze sharpens and focuses on my pussy.

I can almost hear his gears turning, so I complete the thought for him. "Crawl to me."

It takes a beat before he registers that I've spoken, but then he slides off the bed to his hands and knees and starts toward me. I get a thrill imagining a collar around his neck. Would he ever wear one for me? Perhaps more visits to the club would encourage him to consider it.

When he reaches me, he stops, his face just level with Percy's knees.

"Closer," I say. Percy widens his legs to give Lance space, and he moves between them, licking his lips as he stares at where Percy and I are joined. Percy's thrusts make lewd squelching sounds from all the cum spilling out of me.

"Do you see what a mess you made?" I say. "My pussy's covered in you, Lance. I'm so fucking dirty because of you."

He smiles and lifts his gaze. "I know. And I'd do it again."

"Not until you clean me up, but you have to wait until Percy's finished. I want you to bend down and watch him fuck me." He leans in a little, but it isn't enough. "Closer, Lance. I want you so close all you see is him fucking me. All you smell is the scent of your mess all over my pussy and his dick now. You're going to clean us both up when he's finished."

"Fuck yes," he says. "I'm so fucking bad, Queen Justine. Punish me. Make me lick all the cum off your pussy."

The anticipation of what's in store makes me want it faster, but I manage to restrain myself. Lance obeys my command, his face so close to my pussy I can feel his breath against my swollen clit. God, I want him to lick it, but it'll be so much more fun if I make him wait.

But that doesn't mean I can't speed things up a little.

"Faster," I whisper to Percy. He obliges, jacking his hips up into me at a more frenetic pace. He shifts his arms and grabs my breasts, tweaking my nipples and rolling them between his thumbs and forefingers until I cry out. I'm near climax just from his fucking, but I know I can't come this way without a little help.

Percy emits soft, rhythmic grunts against my shoulder, then his grip tightens on my breasts and he roars as he comes. He thrusts deep and hard once more, holding tight as his cock shoots into me. I grip the back of the sofa, my feet twisted behind his ankles to hold on and remain still until his spasms subside and he relaxes. Then I slowly ease up until his cock slips out of me.

A gentle flood runs out of me, and I'm careful when I move, bending both knees and raising my booted feet to rest them on each of Percy's knees, spreading myself even wider for Lance to take his turn again.

His face is flushed, eyes feverish and wild, but he doesn't move. He only looks at me, his gaze requesting permission.

I smile down at him. "Clean us up now. Start with Percy."

He swipes a tongue along one side of Percy's half-hard dick. Percy shudders and presses his face into my shoulder, but doesn't move. By the time Lance has licked every inch of him, he's hard again.

"My turn," I say.

"Hell yeah," Lance murmurs, then presses his mouth over my soaked pussy with a groan. He grips the backs of my thighs and pushes, and Percy takes over, grasping behind my knees to hold my legs wide.

The first sweep of Lance's tongue through the mess makes me lose my mind, but he's nothing if not determined to be thorough. He sucks my clit gently first, then begins working his tongue around my slick flesh, making sure to get into every sensitive hidden place. Then he pushes three fingers into me, fucking while he teases his glorious tongue around my clit.

"Lance! Oh my god, yes!" I'm in heaven, and it only sends me higher when he reaches his free hand up to tease my breasts.

"Don't forget her ass," Percy says, the heat of his words tickling my ear and sending a jolt of ecstasy through me.

Lance hums in acknowledgment and removes his fingers from my pussy, sliding his tongue down to tease around my anus while rubbing my clit with his thumb. He laps at me hungrily and swallows every drop of cum the two of them filled me with, returning to my clit and finger-fucking me again when he finishes tonguing my ass.

The pleasure builds slowly at first, rising only incrementally from the precipice fucking them for so long left me at, but when Lance dedicates his full attention to my clit, it pushes me all the way to the edge.

But he holds me there, slowing his licks while teasing his fingertips against my G-spot oh-so deftly. I surrender, and I'm on the verge of begging, even though that would be completely contrary to the dynamic I wanted to establish.

Lance senses my need somehow, looking up from between my legs and meeting my gaze with a wicked glint in his eyes. He strokes my inside walls in just the right way and gives my clit a playful flick, then a suck.

"I want to fucking drown in you. Squirt your tasty cum all over my face, Gwen. Give it all to me, okay?"

Then he sucks my clit into his mouth once more, tongue dancing around and around until my head is spinning. The orgasm surges through me in a violent rush, and I'm grateful for Percy's arms clamped around my thighs and torso, holding me tight. His mouth is against my ear, urging me on when I let loose, my climax exploding from me along with every ounce of my juices that always seem to flood out of nowhere when I come this hard.

"That's right, give it up for him. He earned it," Percy says. "Next time it's my turn to bathe in you, though."

I'm shaky from all the exertion when Percy's grip on me relaxes, but Lance is still gently licking me, as if he's been told he had to clean his plate and has taken it to heart. I reach down and comb my fingers through his sweat-damp hair, then cup his cheek.

"Good boy," I say in a breathless, passion-roughened voice.

The look of utter adoration he gives me then means *everything*, and I'm positive there's no way I'll ever let this beautiful young man go.

CHAPTER SEVENTEEN

GWEN

The three of us barely move for several seconds. Percy relaxes his hold on me, cradling me on his lap. I reach for Lance, pulling him closer. He surprises me by resting his cheek on my bare thigh while he curls his arms around my waist. I gently comb my fingers through his hair until his heavy breathing slows.

When Percy nuzzles my cheek and presses a kiss to my jaw, I look at him. He's giving me the tenderest of looks and it makes my heart somersault.

"This makes you happy, doesn't it?" he asks.

"Very much," I admit. "It's surprising, but I was definitely losing interest in our scenes at the club."

"Do you want to stop attending the Masquerade?" he asks.

I look down at Lance and shake my head. "Maybe we just evolve. Chloe's usually open to suggestions about the regular live shows. Ours pulls a crowd already."

Lance sits up and looks at me. "Are you suggesting what I think you are? Aren't I blacklisted or something?"

"Oh, you'll have to get the third degree from Chloe, but

I'm sure she'll love you as much as we do," I say. I immediately bite my tongue, schooling my expression as if I didn't just suggest I have feelings too soon. Not to mention I lumped Percy into the statement without even asking.

"Let's not get ahead of ourselves," Percy says with a chuckle. "He gives good head, but I need to get to know him better before pulling out the L-word. But I think this dynamic is exactly what the club needs. Chloe's bound to love the idea."

Lance is staring at us in shock. "Are you serious? Like, I'd be a regular, um, *performer* there? Like Brit and Casey?"

It's my turn to be shocked. "You know them?"

"They share a room in my residence hall. One of them dropped a Masquerade invitation in the lobby on Saturday. That's how I found out about the place to begin with. Man, I had *no idea* what those two got up to on weekends. They're both so dialed in at school."

I'm speechless, but Percy fills the silence.

"They both have very devoted Doms. Slacking in school is probably not allowed if they want to keep coming to the club."

"Is it like, their job? Isn't that…"

He scrunches his forehead, trying to wrap his head around the idea.

I shake my head. "It isn't prostitution, but we are *technically* sex workers. Though Brit, Adam, and Michael don't get paid. Michael's loaded so they just do it for fun. Max, Rick, and Casey earn a salary and so does Percy. I wouldn't let Chloe pay me, since I consider my monthly visits therapy."

"You should get on the payroll," Percy says. "You bring in revenue. It would be a good supplement." He squeezes my hip. "And she'd pay you too," he says to Lance. "She might want you to go through a trial period first, though."

Lance stares at us both, his hair a disheveled mess from my stroking. His bewilderment is endearing as hell, and I can see his gears turning.

"You're on scholarship, but that won't cover law school, will it?" I say.

He nods, but doesn't say anything. I shift on Percy's lap and rest a hand on Lance's shoulder as I stand. "You can think about it. If you like the idea, we'll introduce you to Chloe and pitch her a scene with the three of us. Now can you two help me out of this getup? My ribs are starting to ache, and I think we all need a shower."

Lance rises to his knees immediately and smiles up at me. "My pleasure."

He unzips the backs of my boots and helps me slide them off, then does away with the garters and stockings. Percy reaches around my waist to unhook the fasteners of my corset, and I can finally breathe again when it comes off. Then they stand, each peeling one of my gloves off and dropping them to the floor. I'm bracketed between both men, very aware of how naked we all are.

Happy doesn't begin to describe how this makes me feel. I feel safe, empowered, *alive*, but also pleasantly exhausted and a little sore in all the best places. And *sticky*.

An unholy noise fills the space between Lance and me, interrupting my enjoyment.

"Was that your stomach?"

He grimaces. "I kind of burned right through the bit of fuel I managed to put in me before coming over. Cafeteria pizza only goes so far."

"I'll order food," Percy says. "I think we could all stand to refuel. Meet you guys in the shower?"

Percy pats me on the bottom, then disappears naked out the bedroom door. I take Lance's hand and lead him to my bathroom. My shower is a decent size, but Lance eyes the claw-foot bathtub beside it.

"Wow, how cool is that?"

"It's nice, but better for leisurely soaks. I'm guessing you can't wait that long to eat, so we'll shelve that thought for next time." I'm at the mirror, pinning my hair up and securing my shower cap while he takes in my bathroom, which was one of the features that I loved most about this house when I bought it. Then I turn the shower on and test the temperature and step inside, pulling him behind me. He crowds close so we're both under the stream, reaching back to close the door behind him and smiling down at me.

I can't help but laugh at how giddy he appears. "You're precious."

"Why, because I'm excited to be here?"

"All the reasons, Lance. You're probably the most pleasant surprise I've had in a very long time."

I grip his shoulders and lean up to kiss him. He closes the distance, wrapping his arms around me and returning the kiss with so much desire I'm breathless when we stop. I'm waiting for him to comment on my headgear, but he just keeps smiling and reaches for my body wash.

He's gentle and thorough, but careful to keep his washing businesslike. By the time Percy returns and steps in with us, I'm lathering soap into Lance's back. We step back to make room for Percy to stand beneath the water. I can't read his expression when he looks at us, but he seems relaxed and self-contained. When he meets my gaze, he smiles.

"Hand me the bodywash," he says.

I do, expecting him to start washing himself, but instead he pours some into his hands and lathers it into Lance's chest.

Lance groans and lets his head fall back. "I could get used to this."

"I don't know how often this will be a thing," I say. "This shower is barely big enough for the three of us."

"Switch," Percy says.

He and Lance swap places, and it's Percy's turn to have two pairs of hands see to his washing. My heartbeat thuds when he looks down at me.

"I didn't forget," he murmurs while I soap up his chest.

"I know. We have time."

He lifts a hand to my chin, urging me to hold his gaze. "You deserve the truth, Gwen."

I study him for a beat, appreciating his earnestness, then nod. "And I trust that you'll tell me when it's time. I never doubted you, Percy. You've never let me down when I tell you what I need."

We rotate twice more to get everyone rinsed. Lance is quiet for the rest of his shower, his manner more subdued and introspective than usual. It hits me how little I really know about him, and I resolve to change that, but for now I chalk it up to low blood sugar.

I'm first out, and I'm dried off and in my comfy pajamas when the doorbell chimes. Rather than wait for the boys—*my* boys—to come down, I carry all the food, plus three plates and sets of silverware, to my bedroom. Because a good Domme sees to the needs of her subs in every way she can.

"Oh, thank fuck," Lance says, eyes brightening and nostrils flaring when I enter with two large pizza boxes, on top of which are the dishes and a large bag I'm guessing contains at least a salad. Percy evidently ordered from our favorite Italian place and knows what I like.

But I make them wait while I cover my bedspread with a

spare blanket I don't mind getting messy. Then we dive in like a trio of ravenous beasts.

It isn't until we slow down that the silence shifts like the calm before a storm. It's a testament to how attuned I am to Percy's moods that I know he's ready to talk.

He sets down his empty plate and rises, disappearing into the bathroom to wash his hands. When he returns, he picks up our empty boxes and plates and stuffs them back into the empty bag they came in. All that remains is our dessert, which he moves to my dresser before settling on the bed again. Lance and I are both leaning against the pillows at the headboard, watching intently as Percy stretches out in front of us, pulling my feet onto his lap.

"You don't want cheesecake?" Lance asks, wistfully eyeing the last untouched container Percy set aside.

"I need to do this first," Percy says.

Lance swallows his last bite of pizza crust, brows drawing together. "You want me to leave? Whatever you're about to lay on us must be pretty heavy, based on that look you've got right now."

"You're part of this now, so no, I want you to stay," Percy says. "Then I think you ought to tell your own story."

Lance goes still and pale.

"Lance? What does he mean?"

"You had to guess I'd do a background check on you, kid," Percy says. "But you've got time to figure out what to say. It might be easier once you've heard my story, if it's any consolation."

CHAPTER EIGHTEEN

PERCY

The feel of Gwen's skin under my palm grounds me as I search for the words I promised her. She sits quietly while I distract myself rubbing her feet. I wonder if she realizes that I'd happily do exactly this for the rest of my life if she'd let me, and it's clear to me that Lance is already just as far gone as I am.

It was a dick move to put him on the spot, but somehow it helps lessen my anguish over sharing. I can't avoid this any longer, not if I want to move forward, to let go of the past once and for all. The drawback of Lance's presence is that I can't skimp on details I might have left out because Gwen already knows what was in my Whitewood personnel file. He doesn't know a single thing about me. Maybe I didn't think this through enough.

So I address him instead of Gwen to start with.

"Before I worked at Whitewood, I was a Navy SEAL." I take a breath and register Lance's suspicious look, then remember the white lie I told him the other day. "I lied to you about being an Army medic. I get too many questions if I tell people the truth right away, and I wanted to be the one asking questions that day."

He shrugs. "Fair enough." He nods for me to keep going, and the fact that he doesn't push helps.

"I can't share all the details of my assignments, but they don't really matter anyway—the where or why, and all that. What matters..." I halt, overthinking whether *any* of this matters in the grand scheme of things. But it's my damage, and the look on both their faces tells me that it's going to matter to them, though how much, I can't say. Will they look at me differently after I tell them?

Gwen leans forward and grips my hand, dragging me up and out of my wallowing in self-doubt. She doesn't say anything, just squeezes and looks at me, her expression telling me that she's with me no matter what. I squeeze back, grateful, and take a breath. Gotta rip the fucking bandage off.

"My last mission was the kind of clusterfuck every team dreads. If something could go wrong, it did. And every-fucking-thing was pretty much fucked, but still within acceptable parameters to continue. It wasn't my call whether to abort, but even if it had been, I don't know if I would have. We all just wanted to get it done because we were being reassigned after.

"But I think everyone has a moment when the dread sets in, when despite all your efforts, there's no fixing what's broken, like trying desperately to reassemble the crumbling pieces while everything falls apart around you.

"My team was tight. We anticipated one another's needs well during every other mission we'd been on, and there were dozens. Enough to recognize when we weren't in sync, which was rare.

"We'd reached our target. The building was supposed to be empty except for a lab the enemy used to build chemical weapons. We were already on our way out. Our demolition tech had set the charges, the timer was ticking down with enough time for us to evacuate. It felt too easy. Like we'd forgotten a step, even though we knew better. We made it out and thought we were in the clear. That was when we heard a baby crying."

Gwen's sharp intake of breath twists the old knife in my gut. I look at her, and she has her hand over her mouth. Lance winces. I force myself to rally just so I can finish the story.

"But it was out of our hands by then. I tried to run back in, but my men held me back. Ten fucking seconds on the clock—not enough time to find her, but we saw her silhouetted in a third-floor window right as the charges detonated."

"Oh god," Gwen whispers. "Percy." She reaches for my hand and I let her take it, squeezing back to let her know I appreciate the gesture.

"The aftermath was… infuriating. I won't bore you with the bureaucratic bullshit. Collateral damage was within acceptable parameters. The mission was a success. But none of my team felt like we'd succeeded. Not when an innocent —*two* innocent lives were lost. We're supposed to be protectors. True, we'd taken lives before, but always in the interest of protecting people like that woman. It took me a long fucking time to stop feeling worthless after that.

"But the worst part was that a few years later I tried to confide in someone for the first time about it. About how damaged I'd been all along. They didn't like how much I kept to myself. I wasn't ready to open up but didn't see any other option if I wanted to keep them in my life. I was in love…" I look at Lance, reminded yet again of the face of the person I once believed was the love of my life, so surely they were the one person I could trust to bare my heart and soul to. "I never got an explanation when they left. They just ghosted me and I was left second guessing every decision I ever made after that."

Gwen tightens her grip on me and I make myself look into her eyes, searching for any sign that she's horrified by what I've told her, but I see nothing but concern, nothing but tenderness. It's still difficult to take a breath.

"This was why Chloe asked you to help me, isn't it?"

I nod. "She's a mind reader for sure, because none of that was in my file and I never told her any of it. Maybe she investigated and learned the truth. I wouldn't be surprised; she seems to just know what her people need." I look at Lance. "This is why I think you need to meet her. Tell her your story. I think she can help."

His jaw clenches and he crosses his arms. "What makes you think I need help?"

"Everyone needs a little help, but especially people like us who've been through trauma. Have you talked about what happened with anyone?"

He gives a jerk of his head. "It's ancient history. Did the therapy. I'm fine. How 'bout that cheesecake now?"

He rises, his motions too stiff and tense to play off that he's not affected by my question. Gwen gives me a baffled look and I shake my head. I only know the broad strokes of what happened to Lance, and it isn't my place to share. But now that I've unloaded my own baggage on the two of them, I suppose I feel like I'm owed some reciprocity.

Which is unfair, even though what happened to me was far more recent than what happened to Lance. Everyone heals in their own time, and healing can't happen without a little work. I always knew I'd have to talk about it, and I *have*, but only to Navy shrinks before now, except for one other person.

Gwen and I watch as Lance flips open the plastic to-go box with the dessert inside, grabs a fork, and starts stuffing bites into his mouth right there.

"Lance. It's okay if you don't want to talk right now," Gwen says in a gentle tone. "But if you don't share that cheesecake, you *will* pay for it, one way or another."

His tension shifts and he cuts a mischievous smile her way. "Oh yeah? What'll you do? Spank me?"

"Watch me." She grins and slips out of bed, padding to the dresser where he stands, holding the fork with one large bite hovering in the air. They do a dance with him dodging her reach several times before she stands back and squares her shoulders.

"Do you want me to punish you in a way you really *won't* like?"

"Such as?" he takes another bite and gives her a challenging grin.

"Like making you watch and not allowing you to touch." She peels her thin pajama top off over her head, then pushes her shorts down her legs.

Lance stops chewing and swallows hard, his eyes avidly scanning her gorgeous body. I get half-hard just from the view I have of her backside. It was all I could see earlier while she was riding me, and I have to say I really love that angle. I scoot back against the headboard to watch things unfold.

"Give me the cheesecake," she commands. "And go sit next to Percy."

Surprisingly he obeys, giving me a contrite look when he climbs onto the bed. I don't think it has anything to do with bogarting our dessert, though.

But Gwen's in charge now, and I doubt she'll bargain with him to get him to tell his story; it isn't her style to leverage sex for something that painful. I don't consider our argument to be the same. For us, it was about honoring the trust we've built with each other, and about moving our relationship to the next level. It's going to take more time for Lance to get there, and I can't blame him for needing more time, even though I hoped he'd share tonight.

Gwen doesn't bother putting her pajamas back on, and is delightfully naked and bearing sweets when she climbs onto the bed and kneels between us.

"Open wide," she says, offering a large bite of cheesecake to me. I happily accept, savoring the sweet, creamy flavor while she feeds another bite to Lance.

She continues to feed us until Lance says, "What about you? You haven't taken a bite yet."

"There's only one fork, and I'm not finished feeding you two."

"So give me the fork," Lance says. "You don't get to be the only one taking care of us. We get to take care of you too."

"I'm the Domme here. This is just how it works," she says in a playful tone.

I chuckle, because even though being the dominant suits her, she's far from the most hardcore of dominants I've witnessed at the club. Even Michael, who is all about obedience and never engages in sadistic behavior, is more hardcore than Gwen. His subs like S&M, so he satisfies them by ordering them to spank each other rather than doing it himself.

Gwen's too gentle for that, and I suspect she's more of a switch than she realizes. She definitely responds when Lance leans forward and reaches right into the container, digging his fingers into the second slice of cheesecake and pulling out a hunk, then leaning close to hold it up to her lips.

"Who says we need a fork?"

CHAPTER NINETEEN

LANCE

*I*t's the sexiest fucking thing I've ever seen when Gwen opens her mouth and lets me feed her cheesecake. With my bare fingers.

She lets out a soft moan of ecstasy while she chews and swallows, and my dick gets hard immediately. I scoop up another blob of the creamy dessert and she opens wide, takes it in, then grabs my wrist and wraps her mouth around my fingers.

"Oh fuck, that's hot," I say, barely aware of Percy taking the container out of Gwen's hands.

When she sucks my fingers clean, he's ready with another bite for her, the fork forgotten. She grants him the same sweet blessing of sucking on his fingers, and just watching it makes me wonder if she's really okay with this. It's not that far from sucking on something else.

But I'll accept whatever I can get, so I feed her again, moving close and watching her face intently while she sucks on my two fingers, swirling her tongue around them while she looks into my eyes. I've already eaten my fill of food tonight, but I'm hungry again—hungry for her. When she releases my fingers, I close in and cover her mouth with mine.

She hooks a hand around my nape, kissing me back with a delicious, creamy plunge of her tongue into my mouth. A few seconds in, she giggles, and I pull away to see Percy smearing mashed cheesecake onto one of Gwen's nipples. He drops his mouth to her breast, and she drops her head back with a moan, so I follow his lead, grab another dollop of the destroyed dessert, and coat her other nipple with it.

My head bumps his and we reposition to a better angle to either side of her. I'm the first one to hazard more exploration, sliding a hand up her thigh and delicately grazing her pussy. She's soaked already and sighs, spreading her legs a little wider.

"God, I didn't think I'd want sex again for days, but I do. You guys are ruining me." Her fingers curl through my hair, stroking in that way she did earlier, like she treasures me. Like she cares for me. It's a feeling I didn't realize I craved until tonight, but I can't fucking get enough of it. I want to make her feel good too, and her reaction to my touch says everything.

My fingers are coated in her juices just from my light strokes through her channel. Her pussy's so hot and soft, and she opens for me when I push into her. I start to fuck while my thumb lands on her clit, rubbing lightly.

Percy rises, leaving her other breast unattended. He's kissing her now, so I move my mouth to her other side, needing to make sure no part of her is neglected.

I'm so absorbed in attending to her, I'm only half-aware of her command to Percy to grab the lube, and it takes another moment to wonder what she's planning to do with it. Then she taps me lightly on the arm.

"Lie on your back, honey. I want to ride you."

"Yes, my queen," I say almost jokingly, but there's no doubt I worship this woman. I should call her a goddess, the way she makes me feel.

I rotate and lie back against her fluffy pillows, staring at her in wonder. I must've been knocked unconscious during that fight the other day, and this has all been some crazy fever dream ever since. It's unreal that this gorgeous woman is straddling me, about to sink down on my hard dick.

But she hovers there, holding me in her hand and rubbing my tip up and down through her slickness until I'm about to beg.

Percy climbs back onto the bed, lube in hand. "You sure about this? We've never done it before. It might be painful."

She lets out a breathy "yes" and looks over her shoulder at him. "I want you both inside me. I know you'll be gentle."

"Then you need to lean over. This is going to take a little while. Lance? Fuck her slowly at first, got it? It's going to be torture, but it'll pay off so good."

"I'm on it," I say. I look into her eyes then. "Let me inside."

She nods, and for the first time since her confession about her attack, she looks vulnerable.

I reach up and cup her face in both hands. "We don't have to. There are other ways to be together. All sorts of other ways."

But she just shakes her head, leaning her cheek against my palm. "I want to know what it feels like to surrender to two men I trust. I guess this is the other side of the coin to finding peace again. Taking what I need from you was only half of it. Giving up control, believing you won't abuse the trust I put in you—it's a risk, but one I want to take. One I *need* to take."

She looks down at my cock, then lifts her hips and slots me at her opening. I drop my hands to her hips, watching intently, pulse pounding while she sinks down my full length until her ass rests tight against me.

"Jesus, you feel amazing," I breathe.

Her lips are parted, her eyes glassy with pleasure when she meets my gaze. "So do you," she says with a quirk of her mouth. Then she leans over and kisses me.

I wrap my arms around her, groaning into the kiss as I tilt my hips to push in, then set a slow rhythm while Percy does his thing. I'm very curious about what exactly he's doing, but it isn't until she releases my mouth and presses her face into my neck with a whimper that I look up at him again.

"What do you need to do?" I ask.

He's intently focused on her ass right now, and only glances up at me for a second. He raises the bottle of lube and drizzles a little onto her ass crack, then coats two fingers and holds them up, the clear, viscous fluid glistening.

"Prepping her tight little ass for my dick. You want to know because you want me to do it to you, don't you?"

I frown, then heat fills my cheeks when I remember begging him to fuck me earlier, a request I made when my world was clouded by pleasure.

He chuckles. "Well, this is how it works. If I had graduated plugs, it would be ideal, but all I've got are these." He raises his hand again, fingers splayed. "I start with one." He closes his hand, leaving his pinky raised, then drops it down, swirls it around Gwen's ass, and pushes it into her.

Gwen sighs against my shoulder and whispers, "Don't stop fucking me, please."

I'm absorbed in the lesson, but start moving my hips again, slow and steady. Percy fucks her with his pinky for a few seconds, then raises his hand again. He fucks her with his index finger, then with his thumb, rotating around at an angle. I clench my ass involuntarily at the phantom sensation of his fingers and what they did to me.

"Does it feel as good to her as it did to me?"

He shakes his head. "It feels good, but not *as* good. Her G-spot is in her vagina. Ours is in our ass. But there are still thousands of nerve endings to play with."

He raises his hand again, coats it in more lube, and holds two fingers up like he did earlier. Then he gently begins to work them into her.

Gwen groans and bites down on my shoulder. The slight twinge of pain just makes me hotter on top of all the other amazing sensations: her pussy clenching and releasing around my cock; her full breasts mashed against my chest; the brush of her hair against my cheek. I tighten my arms around her and put my mouth to her ear.

"I've got you. We're going to take care of you, I promise. It'll be so good."

She relaxes and sighs, her pussy unclenching.

"That's a good girl," Percy says. "Stay relaxed." He looks at me. "The most important thing is not to clench while it's happening. That'll just make it hurt more. Believe it or not, your ass can stretch pretty far. It's deeper than a woman's vagina, too."

"That's a trip," I say, my attention wavering due to the change in sensation after her muscles let up their grip. Her pussy feels ten times softer now, and wetter, if that's possible. I force myself to focus on Percy again, because otherwise I'll come too soon. I want to last to see this through.

He withdraws his hand, lubes up again, then pushes three fingers into her.

"How are you feeling, Gwen?" he asks.

"So good," she moans.

Percy chuckles. "I thought so. You have the most perfect

ass. Fucking this tight hole is going to feel so good. We're going to fill both your holes with our cum all night long. I can't fucking wait."

But he still takes his sweet time. I'm not even sure how long it's been since we started, but I'm aching to finish. If nothing else, this whole experience has been a lesson in endurance.

He's up to four fingers, and Gwen's a quivering, moaning mess on top of me. This time I can feel the pressure of his fingers in her ass against my cock, and it wakes me up to what's coming.

He's still finger-fucking her ass when he squirts more lube over the tip of his erection and strokes his cock to coat it thoroughly. Then he gives me a nod, and I slow down and nearly stop. I bring my hands up to urge Gwen to look at me.

"I've got you," I say, staring into her eyes. She's barely hanging on, and the absolute transformation that overcomes her when Percy starts to fuck her ass is fucking beautiful.

CHAPTER TWENTY

GWEN

I'm already a slave to sensation from the deliberate, methodical attention Percy's taken to make me ready. Lance's slow, easy fucking has done the job of keeping me at the edge. He's devoid of body hair, a feature of being a competitive swimmer, which means there's nothing keeping my clit from rubbing against his pelvis every time he thrusts up into me.

But when Percy withdraws his fingers and I feel the hot, blunt tip of his cock pressing into me, every single nerve in my body lights up. Lance holds my face between his hands, staring into my eyes. It grounds me, despite the sense that every cell in my body is on the verge of exploding into pure light.

I hover at the razor's edge, clinging to Lance and grateful that he paused long enough to let me breathe. Then he glances over my shoulder, and at the same time Percy pushes deeper, Lance tilts his hips. His face transforms too, mouth falling open and a soft curse escaping.

"Fuck, I can feel you inside her too," he says.

"I know. It's good, isn't it?" Percy grips my hips as he

buries his cock deep. I'm paralyzed between them, my pleasure stretched to its breaking point.

"Talk to me, Gwen," Percy says. "I won't start moving until you're ready."

Lance raises his eyebrows, still studying my face. "You ready?"

I let out an anxious laugh. "No way I was prepared for this. I'm going to come if either of you move another muscle."

Lance grins. "That makes two of us."

"That makes three of us," Percy adds with a laugh. "But that's what you wanted, isn't it?"

I bite my lip and nod, then look over my shoulder at him. He's just as flushed and wild-eyed as Lance, sweat beading on his forehead, but he isn't moving. I drop my forehead to Lance's shoulder and close my eyes.

"Fuck me as hard as you fucking can. Don't you dare stop until I beg for mercy."

They groan in unison and obey, slamming into me hard and fucking in a frenzy of thrusts, slaps, and grunts. My orgasm hits me almost instantly and persists for what feels like an eternity. In reality, it probably only lasts a minute or two, but the entire universe opens up within my body, exploding into stars and comets and new galaxies.

It's their orgasmic grunts and yells mixing with my hoarse cries that makes it all feel real again, their clutching hands and sticky skin against mine, and Lance's seeking mouth grasping at my lips and holding me hostage in a searing kiss that lasts until the final tremor subsides.

I go limp atop his chest, panting and spent, not even caring about the sticky wetness and the slick sweat pooled between us amid remnants of cheesecake. Percy carefully withdraws from me, leaving me feeling empty, yet completely full at the same time.

"Don't move," he says, disappearing into the bathroom. Lance and I both let out weak chuckles.

"As if I could," Lance says. He strokes both hands down my back and rests them on my ass. "As if I'd want to." He heaves a sigh, then nuzzles against my temple. "Was that good?"

"So good. Gold stars for you both." I'm barely coherent, but gratified by the squeeze he gives my ass.

"Do you hurt?" he asks, one finger gently probing farther, then lightly stroking over my sensitive opening. He's still inside me, and the touch makes me quiver and clench when fresh pleasure floods my already overwrought system.

"No. Just sore from how intense it was, but that's what I wanted." I turn my head so I can see his face. He cranes his neck to look at me, our noses nearly touching.

"You wanted it to hurt?"

I smile and shake my head. "No, I wanted you both to fuck me hard enough to leave a mark. I want to feel it for longer than a day. Long enough to blot out any other memories when I go back to my office. Not that what we did there didn't help, but just in case that wasn't enough."

"Makes sense."

Percy returns with a damp wash cloth and climbs up behind me again, then begins to gently rub the warm cloth between my cheeks.

"Lift and let me get the rest of you," he says.

I obey, finding the strength to rise onto hands and knees, a little sad at having to finally lose the comforting weight of Lance's cock from inside me.

Percy cleans me, then carefully wipes down Lance's flaccid

cock. I shift to the side, falling against the pillows in the middle of the bed and draping my leg across Lance's hips. He cradles me against him with a very satisfied sigh while Percy disappears back into the bathroom and turns on the water.

Lance is silent for a moment, tracing the side of my arm with his fingertips where it's draped across his chest. His touch turns agitated after a moment, and I look up to see a deep frown on his face.

"What is it, honey?" I ask, reaching up to swipe my thumb across the lines beside his mouth. That's when I see the wetness pooling in his eyes, on the verge of spilling free. I sit up more. "Oh, baby, talk to me. Please."

He takes a shaky breath and looks at me, pure agony filling his eyes. "My mom… she died when I was six."

I remain silent while he confesses every memory from his dark, traumatic past, my heart breaking over and over for the child he was and the mother he lost. It wasn't an easy loss, if there is such a thing. She died a violent death, one that could have been avoided if the police had done their jobs.

What's worse was that both Lance and his brother had to bear witness to the entire event, had to watch while masked carjackers forced their mother to pull to the side of the road in a secluded area of town, dragged her out, raped her, then murdered her. They tossed her sons out into the ditch with their mother's bleeding body and left with her car.

He doesn't share the most infuriating part of the event, though—that in all likelihood, the fact his mother was a minority meant the attackers were never caught, or that the police dragged their feet on ensuring justice was served. To them, she was just a statistic. Another casualty of a gang war.

Percy silently hovers in the bathroom doorway for a moment while I cradle a sobbing Lance against my chest. He reads my stricken expression and silently leaves the room.

He knows one angle of the story already, but I doubt he knew how deeply the wound still festered in our boy. I imagine he regrets pressuring him about it earlier. But sometimes healing can't truly begin until the wounds are bared to the light, and all of us have done our share of that this week.

I hold him until his breathing evens and he's worked his way through my box of tissues. He finally looks around and frowns.

"Where's Percy?"

"He left to give us privacy. You can always talk to both of us, you know. Everything we share with each other stays between us, I promise."

"I'm kind of annoyed he left, actually. He's the one who wanted me to talk."

"I doubt it was curiosity that made him press. Misery just loves company. Don't feel like you need to repeat the story for him."

He sighs and shakes his head. "I've talked about it enough. This is the first time I've, um…" He gives me a sheepish look and rakes a hand through his hair. I offer a comforting smile. "It's never been easy to open up about it. You make it easier."

"Do you think the fact that Percy shared his story helped too?"

"Yeah. Do you mind if I go find him? I think I owe him an apology or something."

"You don't, but go ahead. His room is downstairs. I need to hop in the shower and wash off this sticky cheesecake residue."

He grins. "That was fun."

He slides off the bed, and I rise to head to the bathroom.

"Gwen, wait."

Before I make it to the door, he grabs my hand and pulls

me to him. His expression has gone serious, his eyes searching mine.

"What is it?"

"Is this… is this real? I mean, I'm not just some fun diversion, am I?"

My heart skips a beat at how earnest he looks. I face him and place my hands on his shoulders.

"You are so many things, but a diversion is not one of them. I want more nights like tonight with you and Percy. Maybe less emotionally fraught, but tonight has meant everything to me. And I don't want to speak for Percy, but I suspect he feels the same."

CHAPTER TWENTY-ONE

PERCY

I'm too emotionally raw to settle down after everything that happened tonight. After showering again, I slip into the kitchen and find the bottle of good whiskey Gwen keeps hidden behind the breakfast cereal. Tea would probably be safer, but I need to dull this feeling a little so I can process it.

Admitting the truth used to be harder for me, but after years of therapy, it's become a bit of a painful habit, like poking a wound just to feel something.

The truth is I'm scared. Terrified of how quickly things have changed this week. Of how little control I have over the trajectory of events. But what terrifies me most is how much I want to surrender to Gwen's desires, and how vulnerable that makes me.

Vulnerable to hurt, sure, but I've been hurt. I can deal with pain. What I'm most scared of is the crazy part. I'm scared of falling in a way I've never fallen before. Because love opens you up to more potential hurt than anything else, and that's the kind of pain that could break me.

A door opening upstairs sends a shiver of awareness

down my spine, then footsteps head toward the stairs—Lance's, not Gwen's, based on the cadence and heaviness of the steps.

Since living here I've become so attuned to her habits, her sounds, that I wake up in the middle of the night if she wakes up to pee. I usually lie awake, staring at the ceiling until I hear her flush and crawl back into bed again. She's been my entire world for months, but until this past week, it was just a job I got paid for.

Now it's so much more. Now there's another person whose well-being is tangled up with hers, and whose happiness is becoming just as big a priority.

I stand and retrieve a second glass from the cabinet, then sit on my barstool again and pour a measure of whiskey into it. When Lance appears in the arch of the kitchen clad in nothing but the jeans he wore earlier, I push the glass toward him.

"We need to talk," I say.

He hesitates, shoving his hands in his pockets and frowning.

"Don't worry, kid. I'm not going to make you relive the past. I want to talk about us." I glance at the ceiling, then at him.

He nods and shuffles in, then settles on the barstool across the kitchen island. I wait for him to take a drink. He grimaces and exhales after swallowing, then his face lights up when the flavor hits.

"Wow, that's good."

"A gift from Chloe on Gwen's birthday a couple months back. We pull it out for special occasions."

"So does this mean tonight's special?"

"You tell me."

He squares his shoulders. "It's pretty fucking special to

me. I kind of don't want it to end. I feel like we've barely scratched the surface, you know? Like there's so much *more*... more than I can conceive of. I want it all, but it's scary too. Like the first time I attempted a high-dive."

I chuckle. "Yeah, it's like that. Scarier, in some ways."

He lifts one eyebrow. "How does anything scare you? Aren't you trained to jump out of planes and shit?"

"Yep." I take a long swallow. "But nothing holds a candle to what I'm feeling now. And you were the catalyst. Your thirst for adventure kind of threw us both. We were in a rut. You shook us out of it, pushed us to look for more. I hope you realize you're a part of it now. Part of us."

"Whether I like it or not?" he adds.

I smile. "Whether you like it or not. But I sure fucking hope you like it enough to stick around."

He takes a deep breath and stares into his glass, rotating it between his fingers on the countertop. Then he spears me with an intense look.

"I owe you an apology for shutting you out earlier, but I need to thank you for pushing. I think I needed it. I'm all-fucking-in, man. Body and soul."

He raises his glass, and I raise mine. We clink them together, then drink, the weight of what we're toasting hanging between us. It's about more than just us, more than our individual feelings for the woman upstairs. We drink in silence for a few seconds, eyes still locked, so I know we're likely on the same wavelength.

"When we find him, you know what needs to happen," I finally say.

His jaw flexes and he holds my gaze, the fire in his eyes evidence that he knows *exactly* what I mean. He doesn't say the words out loud; he just nods and offers a grim smile.

"I'm right there with you."

The three weeks that follow prove the sincerity of Lance's pledge. He nags his brother daily for updates, but results are slow to come. Ambrose has to use back channels to get access to the intel he needs, which mostly consists of security cam footage from around campus on the night of Gwen's attack.

When he hits a roadblock, he calls me, and I head to the campus security building to see whether I can grease any wheels. I'm not above resorting to threats to get what we need, but it turns out the university's head of security was on the Teams, and he sends the footage over to Ambrose after only a short conversation.

We narrow it down to faculty who had access to the building that night. After-hours, only those individuals with security badges can enter, though it's always possible someone else snuck in. But the possibility of it being a stranger is slim, so I start scrutinizing every male professor who keeps office hours in the same building.

It takes another conversation with the security team to procure a list of people who actually used their badges that night, which narrows things down even more. Finally, Ambrose comes to us with a list of half a dozen names.

"If I give this to you, I need you to promise not to go vigilante on me, okay?" he says when he visits Gwen's brownstone to deliver the list. She and Lance are both still on campus, and since he's taken some of the load of sticking by her side off me, I opted to meet Ambrose alone.

"It never crossed my mind," I lie, reaching for the thumb drive he holds.

He releases it, and it's all I can do not to run to my laptop and open the files.

"I hope you know how much I'm putting my neck out for you three. But I can't just start questioning these men without the chief nailing me to the wall for it, so this is where I need you to do more legwork. Try to engage these men in conversation when you can, casually steer questions to the day of the attack, gauge their reactions when you start to poke. If they start to sweat, that's a good sign they're hiding something."

"I'm trained in interrogation tactics," I tell him.

He narrows his eyes. "This isn't a war zone; it's a college campus. Nobody's getting waterboarded."

I scowl. "No one's getting tortured."

For obvious reasons, I keep to myself the pact that Lance and I made, grateful he isn't here. I don't know how much he's shared with his brother, but from conversations we've had in the hazy aftermath of sex, I've gathered they're close. I hope he'd know better than confess murderous intent with his cop brother, though.

The only misgivings I have is that we're keeping our pact from Gwen, but I don't want her burdened with it. All I want is for the man who hurt her to get what's coming to him.

But I still haven't opened the file after he leaves. I sit with a drink instead, staring at it while I wait for Gwen and Lance to get back.

Lance spent most nights with us the first week after the night of confessions, but since then has forced himself to study on campus most weeknights and on days he has to train. I admire his dedication to both his studies and his swimming career. He'd have made a fine SEAL, had he chosen that route instead. Some afternoons Gwen and I meet him at the pool, and she cheers us on while we race. He kicks my ass every time.

Halfway into my drink, I realize I can't stop thinking

about them both and my dick is hard. I raise a hand to touch the chain hanging around my throat, a gift from Gwen this past weekend. It's a medium-weight gold with a larger circular link that hangs in front—her version of a collar for me to signify our relationship. Lance has a similar collar, but his is silver. Thankfully it's adjustable, so I can loosen it enough to hang below the neckline of a shirt, but today it's cinched like a choker.

We've scheduled a meeting between Lance and Chloe the evening of the next Whitewood Masquerade, which is this weekend. After all the fun we've had, I can't wait to experience our dynamic in a new setting—with observers, assuming Chloe is on board.

When Gwen's key slides into the lock of her front door, every cell in my body ignites. It's crazy how much I get off on the very idea of what we now are to each other, of how well we fit, and of how much I crave them both when they're away for any length of time. Solitude hasn't been something I've had a lot of recently, though, so maybe there's some truth to that old adage that absence makes the heart grow fonder.

I finish my drink and meet them at the door, pulling Gwen into a kiss, then sharing one with Lance the second the door closes behind them. The flash drive sits forgotten on the counter for the time being; I have other priorities.

CHAPTER TWENTY-TWO

GWEN

*T*his new version of Percy is a delightful change, and one I'm still getting used to. I've lost count of the number of times I've arrived home after being separated from him, only to have him fall to his knees in the foyer and strip my panties down my legs until he can get to my pussy.

"Wow, you weren't joking, were you?" Lance says, laughing at the ravenous beast wearing Percy's skin. He has my skirt shoved up to my hips and my panties around my knees while he tongues my clit.

I moan and let my head fall back against the door, looking at Lance through half-lidded eyes. It isn't as if I've discouraged Percy from this kind of greeting—quite the opposite.

"It's not so bad," I say, then let out a squeak of surprise when Percy lightly nips my labia with his teeth.

He looks up at me with a wicked gleam, then to Lance.

"Don't blame me for missing you both." He reaches for Lance, rubbing along the front of his jeans until his cock swells, then yanking at the button. Percy keeps a hand at my pelvis, thumb toying with my clit while he tugs Lance closer by his waistband and unfastens his fly, then pulls out his stiff cock. He leans over to take the swollen mushroom tip into his mouth.

It's Lance's turn to groan, and when he braces a hand against the door next to my head, I reach up and grip his forearm. He shifts his gaze from Percy to me, then leans in and kisses me.

Percy's tongue returns to my clit, the slick sounds of stroking betraying the slide of his hand on Lance's cock. Lance and I continue our kiss while his free hand roams my chest, squeezing one breast and thumbing my nipple through the fabric. He lets out a frustrated noise and grabs the bunched-up hem of my dress, yanking it up. The stretchy fabric slips over my head easily, and he wastes no time tugging the front of my bra down so both cups push my breasts up and together.

"That's more like it," he says, grinning as he fondles me, then resumes our kiss. We're both moaning into each other's mouths while Percy services us, this doubled attention a new adventure. With Lance staying on campus half the time, it's usually just me and Percy drowning in each other over missing our third. Lance has made it a habit to walk me home, but usually—very reluctantly—he turns around and heads back to campus without coming inside. This is the first time in a while he and I have returned home together.

Percy lifts one of my legs and drapes it over his shoulder to gain better access, pushing two fingers into my aching channel and finger-fucking, the rhythmic sound keeping tempo with the wet staccato of his fist on Lance's cock. I don't know how they both do it, but they're masters at giving me the most intense, explosive orgasms I've ever had. I've had to stop being worried about drenching their clothes, because they don't seem to care. If they did, they'd take their shirts off.

"I'm gonna fucking come," Lance murmurs, mouth pressed against my throat. He groans and bucks at my side, his desperate sounds driving me closer too.

Percy's mouth leaves my pussy briefly. "Do it. Come on me. I want to be covered in both of you. I want to fucking bathe in you."

His hunger is palpable as he takes Lance in his mouth again, his hand still working at my pussy, fingers buried in me while he rubs my clit with his thumb.

Lance squeezes my breast and lets out a pained grunt, then throws his head back. "Fuck!"

I'm at the razor's edge, mesmerized by the sight of Percy pulling his mouth off Lance's shaft and milking streams of semen from him. Lance's creamy spend hits Percy's mouth, his cheek, his chin, and Percy uses the tip to spread it around his lips and over his tongue before turning back to me.

"Oh god," I moan when he covers my pussy again with his filthy, cum-covered mouth. "You are such a dirty boy."

He chuckles as he tongues me, pausing only to glance up and say, "You love it."

"God I do. I love you both for how filthy you are with me."

Lance is breathing hard, face flushed from his climax as he leans against the door, watching Percy tongue my pussy. He idly reaches down and swipes a finger through one of the splatters of semen on Percy's cheek, then raises it to my lips.

"Dirty enough for you?" he asks, smearing his semen over my mouth. Then he leans in and kisses me deep and hard, dropping his wet fingertip to my nipple and coating it in what remains. I moan at the jolt of pleasure the salty flavor of his spend sends through me, magnifying the already overwhelming ecstasy of Percy's tongue against my clit.

I climax in a sudden rush, the sensations flooding me just

like the built-up fluid floods Percy's tongue, drenching his chin and dripping down his chest. He continues languidly licking like he wants to swallow every drop, until the leg I'm still standing on starts to shake and buckle. I laugh as I slide down the door, and Percy catches me, falling back on his ass and hauling me onto his lap.

"Easy there," he says. "How was your day, baby?"

Lance drops down to join us, leaning back against the doorjamb, his pants still undone and his half-hard cock jutting out of them, pressed against his lower abdomen by his boxers.

"Does he greet you like this every time you come home?" he asks. "'Cause if so, I need to move in or something."

"Only since the two of you have started splitting babysitting duties," I say.

"Don't call it that," Lance protests. "You're not a baby. We're your bodyguards—body *servants*. Basically anything your body needs, we're here to give you."

"What he said," Percy replies, shifting me on his lap and grimacing. I'm suddenly very aware of the rigid lump in his jeans.

"Hold on, we aren't finished here, are we?" I slip to the side and reach for his belt. He grabs my wrist.

"That isn't necessary."

"Aw, to hell it isn't," Lance says, reaching for him too. "You got us *both* off in a matter of minutes. That takes serious talent—talent that should not go unrewarded."

I unfasten Percy's belt, and Lance handles his button and zipper while I push Percy back, smiling as he stretches his legs and lowers himself to the floor. Lance even goes as far as to grab Percy's waistband and yank his jeans down his legs, then off over his bare feet.

Seeing him prone in front of me, staring up at me with

pleading eyes, reminds me of how much I love when either of them surrender like this. His pleasure is entirely in my hands now, and I reach for his stiff cock while still watching his face.

I wrap my hand around him and give a gentle stroke, gratified by the way his lips part around a quick exhale before sucking in another breath. When I squeeze, he lets out a needy groan and stretches his arms over his head, fingers grasping at the legs of a sofa table just beyond the entry.

"You hold him, I'll suck him," Lance suggests.

He bends one of Percy's strong legs at the knee and positions himself between them, then cups Percy's balls and fondles before lowering his mouth to the tip of Percy's cock.

I keep hold of the shaft while Lance sucks and licks the tip until Percy's hips begin a slow undulation to the rhythm. When I look at him, his eyes are closed, his cheeks colored by a high flush.

My heart skips a beat at how beautiful he looks right now—angelic, really—with his gold hair haloing his head and his gold choker resting against the pulse at the side of his throat. He's earned a bit of dedicated attention after what he just did, and an idea creeps into my head unbidden, sending my own pulse racing with a combination of fear and elation.

I release his cock and squeeze Lance's shoulder. "Let me have a turn."

Lance sits up, eyes wide. "You mean, like… with your mouth?"

"Yes." My voice is weak, breathless, and it's hard to pull air in, but I want this, no matter how scary it is.

Percy tenses and pushes up onto his elbows. "Gwen, you don't have to. Neither of you have to."

His protest galvanizes me. I turn to him and shake my head. "I know. But I want to." I scoot closer and rest my hand on his chest, peering down into his eyes so he knows I mean it. "I want to make you feel as good as you make me feel. I'm tired of just watching Lance do it all."

His brows draw together with worry and he lifts a hand to cup my cheek. "I don't want you to feel obligated. Ever. Promise me it's what you want, okay?"

His earnestness makes me smile, and I nod. "I promise."

I bend over and kiss him, savoring the moment and the bubble of warmth and love inside me. I wasn't lying when I said I loved them, and not just because of what filthy beasts they turn into sometimes. I adore them. Sometimes the immensity of what I feel for them is so great it frightens me. So I want this, as much to return some of the attention he gives as to take one more step to banishing my traumatic memories.

When he releases me, I move slowly down his body, pushing his shirt up above his nipples to flick my tongue around each one in turn. He moans and gently threads his fingers through my hair. I still, jolted from the moment by the sensation of his big hand on my head.

"Sorry," he says, yanking it back. "You might want to tie me up, if you don't want me touching you while you do this."

I shake my head. "I trust you. I'm still figuring out what triggers me."

Lance is still kneeling between Percy's legs, watching intently as I continue down Percy's torso, teasing my tongue along the concave furrow between his abs. His hair tickles my lips, and my heartbeat quickens as I approach my target. He must have freshly showered before we got home, because the spicy scent of his bodywash permeates my nose, only mildly spiked with the musky aroma of *him*.

"You've got this," Lance says softly, holding Percy's shaft in his fist. "Baby steps, right? He likes it if you lick him here."

He grazes his thumb up the underside of Percy's cock, swiping through the sheen of wetness coating his frenulum.

I take a breath and bend down, giving a tentative lick to the length of skin Lance indicated.

Percy lets out a breathy chuckle. "Fuck yeah, I love that."

Percy's flavor coats my tongue, an almost instant aphrodisiac. I've tasted him many times in the past few weeks, though it was always limited to the remnants on Lance's tongue or fingers. The familiarity of it makes it easier to do it again, this time with less trepidation. Percy is flat on his back, after all, both hands white-knuckled around the legs of the table.

So I take his head fully between my lips and give a light suck, swirling my tongue around and around. I'm not new to blowjobs; I'm just cautious not to wake the victim still cowering inside me, terrified of letting herself be overpowered by a man again. But this is very different than the last time I had a penis in my mouth. This is mostly for pleasure, and only partly power and control. I love that Percy's at my mercy, but making him feel good is my primary focus.

When I pull off, I'm already craving more. "Share with me," I say to Lance.

He grins. "Hell yeah."

Then we both press our mouths to Percy's hard cock, one on either side. I run my tongue down his length and back up while Lance sucks, then we trade places.

"Holy fuck," Percy mutters, staring down at us while we tease him.

"You earned it, brother," Lance says. He puts two fingers in his mouth, coating them with saliva, then drops them between Percy's legs. "Now we're going to make you come as hard as you made us."

I'm still marveling at how much I'm enjoying this after

fearing it for so long, but pause long enough to watch while Lance pushes his fingers into Percy's ass. Percy's cock kicks in my hand and he groans, letting his knees fall wider.

"God, that's it. Fuck me. Suck me. Do whatever the fuck you want."

"Do you want to swallow him when he comes?" Lance asks. I pause my sucking to think about it, then nod and resume. I'm committed to seeing this through, now that it's begun.

After that, muscle memory takes over. I stroke and suck, taking him deep enough to test my gag reflex. Lance jacks his fingers into Percy's ass, fondling his balls with his other hand while Percy groans and fails to restrain his undulating hips.

He barely gets out what I know is a warning for my sake. "Holy fucking *fuck!* I'm coming!"

I suck harder, making sure I have him all the way to the hilt when his cock begins to erupt, bathing the back of my throat with his semen.

Even though *he* was the one coming, my entire body tingles as I swallow every drop, and when I slide my lips off, I kiss his tip.

Then I realize tears are streaming down my face.

CHAPTER TWENTY-THREE

GWEN

*P*ercy's heavy breathing halts, and he sits up suddenly.

"Gwen? Baby, what's wrong?" He cups my face in his hands and tilts my head, staring into my tear-fogged eyes. "Talk to me. Are you okay?"

I nod and give him a shaky smile. "I did it." I sniffle and look between him and Lance. The latter's stricken expression eases, and Percy huffs out a breath, hauling me onto his lap.

"Fucking hell, you scared me. No blowjob is worth worrying about traumatizing you."

I wipe my wet face on the tail of his shirt and laugh softly. "You didn't traumatize me. It was my choice—*my choice*. And it felt so good to make *you* feel good for a change. I got overwhelmed with happiness, I guess. That's all."

He stares into my eyes, still skeptical. I place my palm against his cheek, then reach for Lance's hand to comfort him too.

"Guys, I promise I'm fine. I feel amazing. But next time, let's do this in a bed, okay?"

Percy tightens his hold on me, then buries his face against

my neck with a groan. "You always make me feel good. Just being around you feels good. Don't you get that?"

I let him hold me while I stroke his hair, the weight of his worry sinking in. "It's different when I can't give you something I know you love. I'm just happy that hopefully won't be an issue from now on. Though I think experimenting with more bondage might be in order, just to keep you in line."

Lance clears his throat and raises his hand. "I volunteer as tribute for the bondage and blowjobs."

Percy and I both laugh. "We'll just have to make that happen, then," I say.

Neither of them have pressured me for oral sex since we started our adventure. We established our ground rules as a threesome the first weekend after Lance spent the night. He was the one who wrote "No BJs from Gwen" on our shared list of hard limits. One of his soft limits was "no receiving anal *yet*," because after Percy explained the preparation needed to take it properly, he got a little squeamish. But with any kinky relationship, it's always best to let the people involved set their own pace and shift their limits when they're ready.

Percy pats me on the butt. "As much as I'd like to do all the things with you two right here and now, this hard floor leaves a lot to be desired. I've got news from Officer Lacosta to share anyway."

Lance's eyebrows shoot up. "Ambrose was here? What'd he have to say?"

"Let me get cleaned up first, then meet me in the kitchen in a bit. There's a thumb drive on the counter with a list of names on it, if you want to take a peek."

He urges me off his lap, but Lance is already on his feet, reaching for my hand, then Percy's. We split up, Percy heading to his room while I run upstairs to put on fresh clothes, and Lance making a beeline for the kitchen.

When I come back downstairs, Lance is leaning over his laptop on the living room coffee table and scowling. When I enter, he moves over to make room for me on the sofa, angling the screen toward me.

"These names are all teachers in the sociology department," he says. "I recognize them, but you probably know more about them than I do."

My stomach turns a flip. But when I scan the names, none of them leap out at me as memorable. They're my colleagues. Some of the names have been struck through, but only those of the women in my department.

"This list isn't the entire staff roster," I comment.

"No, these are just the names of the people who accessed the building with their keycards the night of your attack. Can you narrow it down at all?"

I frown, forcing myself to focus on one name at a time.

Wentworth Davis
Conrad Weltz
Heath Sopel
Philip MacArthur
Damon Banio
Emil Tong

My vision blurs, panic welling too fast to process. I slam the screen shut and sit back.

"I can't. I'm sorry." I cover my face with both hands, struggling not to burst into tears at how paralyzed I am by this very simple task. One of these men *raped* me. It doesn't matter where he stuck his dick; it was rape.

A big hand squeezes my shoulder and Percy settles on the sofa next to me.

"Let me see the list," he says. He lifts the laptop screen

again while I sit back, watching his fingers swipe the trackpad. His hands, so strong, yet gentle, have been there for me through so much. I take a deep breath, inhaling his warm, freshly showered scent, and my heartrate gradually slows.

When Lance entwines our fingers and squeezes my hand, I look at him with a grateful smile.

"We'll figure it out together," he says.

"We can eliminate three of these names at least," Percy says. "Damon Banio is Black, and you said the hands of the man who attacked you were white. Wentworth Davis is old as fuck and never leaves the first floor of the building. And Heath Sopel is trans—pre-reassignment. He doesn't have a dick."

"This is good," Lance says. "So we just have to interrogate three assholes. I have Law in Societies with Dr. Tong on Monday. Want me to try to talk to him after class?"

I sit up, a thought occurring to me. "The department mixer."

Both men look at me like I'm speaking in tongues. "The cocktail party this weekend at the dean's house. They do one every year for new majors and prospective grad students to network and kiss up to the faculty. I was going to skip it, since it's on the same night as the next Whitewood Masquerade, but all these men will be there. One thing they all have in common is that they love to kiss Dean Robertson's ass."

Lance's eyes light up. "Right! I got an invitation too, since I'm graduating in May."

"I can talk to Chloe," Percy says. "She can adjust the schedule for us in case we need to arrive late. Or make arrangements if we need to cancel."

He studies me with a frown, and I realize he's trying to gauge my potential for being a basket case after we identify my attacker—assuming we're able to figure out who it was. I shake my head.

"If anything, I'm sure I'll want the outlet. Besides, it'll be Lance's official introduction to the club, so we can't skip it."

But neither man looks enthusiastic. They lock gazes, and something indecipherable passes between them. Something that raises alarms and makes the hairs on the back of my neck stand on end.

"What was that about?"

Lance averts his gaze and reclaims his laptop, closing his apps and turning it off.

"Nothing for you to worry about," Percy says, standing and walking away. "I'm going to start dinner."

I stare after him in shock, then at Lance. "Don't you dare shut me out. What are you keeping from me?"

He glances toward the kitchen, his jaw clenching. "I can't tell you," he says, giving me a beseeching look.

"The hell you can't. Secrets aren't allowed, especially if it has anything to do with me, and I have a feeling whatever you two are hiding is *all* about me. Tell me."

"Gwen, don't…"

"God*damnit*, Lance! What are you guys keeping from me? Is it about him? Do you know something already?"

"No… we just…" He heaves a sigh and looks at the ceiling. When he meets my eyes again, his expression is fierce. "They never caught the men who raped my mother, you know. They identified the weapon by the bullets they shot her with. Found the gun in the aftermath of a gang war a couple years later and just wrote it off, concluding her attackers were two of the casualties of that bloodbath." He shakes his head, lips pursed like he's tasted something bitter. "My brother and I never really got justice. For all we know, they could still be alive."

His confession derails my outrage briefly, and I deflate. "I'm sorry, I didn't know."

"I want you to have justice, Gwen. The man who hurt you … he doesn't deserve to breathe the same air as you."

An icy chill spreads through my limbs. I shake my head in disbelief. "No."

"You deserve no less," he says, a determined set to his jaw. "I will never get to see the light leave the eyes of the men who hurt my mom, but I can do this for you. *We* can do this for you."

Percy reappears from the kitchen, glowering at Lance. When he looks at me, he blinks, uncertainty filling his expression.

"Do you really believe I'd want the two of you to commit *murder* for me? You'd be throwing your lives away!"

"Not if we don't get caught," Percy says. "We aren't idiots."

Hot rage replaces the chill of realization. "That's *exactly* what you are, if you thought I'd want this! I want payback, yes, but not at the price of your futures—or the price of *our* future. Did you even fucking *think* about what could happen? I could lose you both if you got caught."

"You know as well as I do that even if we turn the fucker in, there's a chance he'll get off. The justice system is fucking broken, and you know it," Lance says.

"I am aware, but I will just have to take that chance. I won't condone you two committing a crime so atrocious for my sake. You'd be no better than him."

They share a look, and then thankfully, Lance nods. "Okay. If you don't want this, then we won't do it. We'll figure out a way to get him to incriminate himself and turn him in. I hope to fuck it works."

When I look at Percy, his arms are crossed and he's

clearly disappointed. I reach for his hand, peeling it away from him to hold. My heart is in my throat.

"I don't need you to do this for me, okay? I appreciate your anger, but the risk is just not worth it. I love you too much to let you compromise your integrity."

He blinks rapidly, his mouth falling open. He looks startled, confused, then hopeful. "Do... Do you mean that?"

"What? That I love you? How could I not, after everything you've done? You're half of my heart now, Percy. Lance is the other half."

I extend a hand to Lance, who is observing silently, an unreadable expression on his face. When I reach for him, his eyes light up. He closes the distance.

"I fucking love you so much," he says, bracketing my face with both hands and kissing me the way he did the night we met.

He releases me just in time for Percy to haul me close, lifting me off my feet to kiss me too.

I wrap my arms around his shoulders, sinking into the embrace, into his kiss, in a way I never have before. He releases me after several seconds, and I rest my forehead against his, laughing breathlessly.

"Wow."

He grins. "Wow is right. God, Gwen, I never thought we'd wind up here. I love you too—so goddamn much it hurts sometimes."

CHAPTER TWENTY-FOUR

LANCE

*Y*ou would think I'd be more comfortable in a jacket and tie, considering my career goals, but no matter how hard I try to make outfits like this work, I still itch. At least Percy looks just as out of sorts in his suit, no matter how well it fits him. He's more polished than I expected, his hair pulled back into a sleek little manbun, not a strand out of place.

"What?" he mutters when he catches me looking at him shortly after we arrive at the mixer. We're awkwardly lingering in a corner while Gwen schmoozes with Dean Robertson.

"You look hot," I say, surprising myself. It's only been within the last week since our love confession with Gwen that I started looking at him more objectively, appreciating his appearance the way I appreciate hers. She's as stunning as always tonight, wearing a backless purple cocktail dress with a high halter neckline.

"Are you wearing the plug?" he asks.

My neck heats. "Fuck no. I'd never be able to concentrate

with something shoved up my ass. If all goes well, I'll..." I clear my throat. "I'll put it in after."

"Better not wait too long, because your ass is mine tonight."

His promise causes sweat to prickle between my shoulder blades. I did make a promise, and even bit the bullet and did all the prep for it, which included a couple tasks I know I'll need to get used to, but that I'm still weirded out by. I got well-acquainted with graduated plugs, for one thing, and the largest one rests heavy in my inner jacket pocket, just waiting until I'm ready for it.

The things I do for love.

The worst part is that I haven't eaten, and I *can't* eat until afterward. As fun as spontaneous butt sex sounds, I didn't miss the fact that Percy immediately went to clean up when we were done that first night. So it's nothing but water for me tonight, which is fine, since I need a clear head if I'm going to interrogate anyone.

"I'm going to go find my target. Hopefully this will go fast," I say. No sense waiting longer than necessary.

"Remember to record the conversation."

"Got my phone set up already." I wave my smartphone at him, the voice recording app ready to go as soon as I can track down Dr. Tong.

He isn't hard to find; his nasally giggle is a dead giveaway. I follow the sound to the kitchen, where he's chatting with another faculty member and a pair of students I recognize. His bespectacled eyes light up when he sees me. I tap the record button on my phone and slip it back into my jacket pocket before approaching.

"Mister Lacosta, I didn't expect to see you here tonight." He reaches a hand out to shake, so I grip it and nod. He's relatively unintimidating in stature and manner, and I've always liked him well enough as a teacher, but I don't want to draw any conclusions yet.

"I'm graduating in a couple weeks. Figured it couldn't hurt to show my face to the graduate faculty."

His eyebrows draw together in mild confusion. "But you're pre-law, aren't you? You should be at the law school mixers."

"Oh, I intend to go to those too. Just making sure I don't burn bridges, you know." I give him what I hope is a confident smile to cover up how utterly full of shit I would be, had I not had an enema a couple hours ago.

"Smart man." He nods sagely. "We'd love to have you stay with us, if that's your choice, but with your grades, I'm sure you'll excel anywhere."

I shrug and try to come up with a few leading questions to gauge the likelihood of him assaulting Gwen. Thankfully he turns to the others and starts to talk me up as if I'm the best thing since peanut butter. I'm waiting for the right moment to interject when another man slips up beside him, sliding a possessive arm around his waist and eyeing me warily.

He sticks a hand out. "I'm Garrett, Emil's husband."

My eyebrows shoot up. I'm dumbstruck for a moment, and it takes a beat before his defensive look sinks in. Evidently, I have absolutely *lousy* gaydar.

"Nice to meet you," I say, bewildered by both Dr. Tong's enthusiasm about me and his husband's attitude.

"Garrett and I saw your last meet. Impressive times!" Dr. Tong says. "Your performance rivals that of Olympic swimmers."

Garrett begrudgingly nods in agreement.

"Oh. Wow. I had no idea you followed college sports, much less swimming."

"It's the outfits," Garrett says, smirking. Dr. Tong elbows him in the ribs and rolls his eyes.

"We get free admission to a few events a semester. Swimming is one of our favorites. Less violent, you know." He wrinkles his nose as if the idea of violence is distasteful.

"It is definitely not a contact sport," I agree.

"So, I have a personal question," he says, adjusting his glasses and leaning a little closer. "I hope this doesn't seem inappropriate, but I wondered if you could settle a little disagreement between Garrett and myself: Are you naturally hairless, or do you shave for meets?"

Garrett groans. "Emil, seriously? You've had *one drink*."

Dr. Tong's eyes widen at his husband. "What? It's not lewd to ask."

I can't help but laugh. "It's okay. I actually wax before every competition."

"Everything?" Dr. Tong asks, his gaze sweeping over me. Man, this guy is *not* subtle when he's buzzed.

"Jesus, I can't take you anywhere," Garrett says.

"Um… yes, actually. It reduces drag. Plus it's a whole psychological prep thing," I say, trying to suppress a laugh.

Dr. Tong tries to ask something else, but Garrett cuts him off. I'm too amused to be offended, but excuse myself when the pair start bickering.

I tap the button to stop recording on my way back through the party, looking for Percy. I find him chatting with his target, Professor Weltz, not far from where I left him. I scan the room, but there's no sign of Gwen. She insisted on doing her part and chose Dr. MacArthur, since she's better acquainted with him than the others.

Not trusting my people-reading skills at all after discovering Dr. Tong is gay, I stand unobtrusively off to the side by a bookshelf, pretending to peruse the selection while I eavesdrop on Percy's conversation. Dr. Weltz teaches Sociological Theory and comes across as a typical academic, complete with the tweed blazer with elbow patches. He's currently bending Percy's ear about Sigmund Freud's theories on sexuality. Percy looks interested, but when I catch his eye, he slow blinks, and I get the distinct sense he's a hostage to the conversation. But nothing about his manner suggests he believes this guy is our man.

Dread settles in my belly, and I'm scanning the room for Gwen when Percy finally extracts himself from Weltz and joins me.

"What's the verdict on Tong?"

"Gay and happily married."

"You heard some of that lecture just now. Weltz is too detached about sex. He's the kind of man who gets off on hearing himself talk. Where's Gwen?"

"Not sure. But if Tong and Weltz are ruled out, we need to find MacArthur."

Percy's jaw spasms and his gaze sweeps the room. "I knew I shouldn't have let her talk to him alone. Let's split up. You look down here, I'll head upstairs."

CHAPTER TWENTY-FIVE

GWEN

I'm buoyed by my conversation with the dean when I head off to find Dr. MacArthur. Dean Preston as good as promised me a better office, and he complimented me on the quality of feedback the department receives every year from the students who take my classes. I stop by the drinks table to pour myself a glass of wine, then wander through the house, positive I saw MacArthur somewhere near the library when I arrived.

Percy and Lance have already split up to go ply their targets with conversation. I try to ignore the little ball of anxiety that flares in my belly and remain detached. One of these men might be my attacker, but I have a hard time imagining any of them doing what was done to me. Is it possible some outsider gained access? Ambrose was cautious when I asked that question, suggesting that yes, it's possible, but not likely; he believed we needed to rule out the people I know first.

The dean's home is fashioned in a modest Arts and Crafts style in a nice neighborhood. I've been here once before, but it was during the winter when it was dark and icy outside and everything was closed up tight. It's early May now and just past sunset, so the French doors at the rear of the house are open to a view of a garden, its stone paths winding through foliage exploding with spring flowers.

When I reach the doors to admire more of the garden, I see Dr. MacArthur in profile, standing at a corner of the path and speaking with someone out of view. I step out, marveling at the intricate landscaping details, and decide I need to ask Dean Preston who did the work out here. I have a small square of yard at the back of my brownstone that I'd love to make as magical as this.

I head toward him, pausing when I remember I need to record any conversation we have, no matter how benign. I'm thrilled my dress has pockets cleverly obscured by the drape of the skirt when I stash my phone in one.

The person he's talking to appears to be a young woman, a student I recognize from one of my classes, who looks distinctly relieved when I come into view.

"Hello, Ms. Brennan," he says, and I have to school my features to obscure my annoyance over the fact that he always fucks up my title.

"It's beautiful out here, isn't it?" I reply. "Such a lovely spring evening."

He nods, cutting his eyes to the student, then back to me, giving me the sense that I'm interrupting something.

"Yes, it is, and what better place to enjoy it than Preston's garden? I was just about to show Bethany the most alluring part. Perhaps you'd like to join us?"

His tone is less than inviting, but Bethany shakes her head. "I really need to pee. Maybe later? Nice talking to you, Dr. MacArthur." She practically sprints toward the house, leaving me staring after her in concern.

MacArthur sighs, and when I look back to him, his smile seems forced. "I hope I didn't interrupt anything," I say.

"Not at all. It's nice to see you, Gwen. I wasn't sure if you would come. You've skipped the last few faculty get-togethers."

"I just haven't been feeling all that social this semester. It's nothing personal, I promise."

He nods and sips his drink, which looks like bourbon. I gesture with my wine glass. "So, where is the most alluring part of the garden you mentioned? I would love a tour, if you know your way around."

"I do. Preston and I are both Columbia alums. I saw the place when he started working on it a decade ago."

"Do you visit in the fall? I imagine it's just as gorgeous then with all these maple trees." It's a clumsy attempt at steering the conversation to the timeframe of my attack, but I have no idea where to take it next. Sociology topics make sense, so I rack my brain for a better question while he leads me around the winding path to a shadowy, secluded area beneath one of those maple trees. Dark flagstones surround a small, oblong koi pond with lily pads floating on its surface. Flowering plants surround two-thirds of the pond, and a small fountain flows into it at the far end. It's stunning.

He pauses by a hand-carved wooden bench while I turn to admire the golden light reflecting off the water. Orange- and white-mottled fish dart beneath the surface.

"It's a different beauty in the autumn. Starker." In a lower voice, he says, "The summer flowers complement you much better, I think."

My skin prickles at his suddenly too-close proximity. He brushes the back of my bare arm with a fingertip, and I freeze. Blinking rapidly to gather myself, I take a breath, inhaling the strong scent of wintergreen—the scent of *him*. My attacker.

"Th-Thank you." I can't move, too overwhelmed with shock. I've worked with this man for years. How could it be him?

Little details flood in from my memory: the times he asked me out and I turned him down; the way I'd find him outside my office on odd occasions, even though his office was at the other end of the building; and the rumors from female students—he was the man Brit and Casey had been gossiping about at the club a few weeks back, but I'd just chalked it up as rumor, given he's attractive and distinguished.

And a predator.

It takes a moment for my head to clear, and for me to stop berating myself for my stupidity and remember why I'm here. I need to keep him talking despite the clammy fear that grips me. I need him to incriminate himself.

"You are so beautiful in that dress, Gwen," he says. His hand rests against the exposed skin of my back, then slides around, *underneath* the fabric. "I can't keep my hands off you."

I grit my teeth, forcing myself to relax when he pulls me back against his body and nuzzles my neck. This close, his scent is overwhelming. Bile rises into my throat.

"Please..." I wince and restrain myself from asking him to stop. I have to keep him talking long enough. "What do you like best about me?" I ask, grimacing at how clumsy a question it is, but he takes the bait.

"Hmm, your soft skin—so delicious. Your curves." His hand gropes upward beneath my dress, and I hold my breath as he pinches one of my nipples through my bra.

The bastard's erection digs into my low back as he grinds against me. I gasp in disgust. I don't want this. Nothing about this feels right. I want to crawl out of my own skin to get away from him, but I can't. Not yet.

Thankfully he releases my breast, but then he spins me around. His hot breath hits my lips, and I cringe at the mix of bourbon and wintergreen. He cups the back of my head.

"I think you know my favorite part is your mouth, Gwen." He digs his fingers into my neck, pulling me closer. "Those full lips. That soft tongue." He grips my chin with his free hand and leans closer. The bastard thinks he's going to *kiss* me!

My hands shoot to his chest and I push back, pulling against his grip at the same time.

"No, I do *not* consent to be manhandled by you! Get off me!"

He pulls harder, smirking. "Come on, Gwen," he coaxes. "You were such a good girl the last time. You got on your knees and took me like a fucking champ. I don't remember you saying no."

"I didn't fucking say yes, either, and you know it."

"It would be your word against mine. I have tenure. Preston is my oldest friend. You might as well just give me what I want."

Like hell I'll do anything this man wants. I hope my phone caught everything he said, because I am *done* letting him touch me like this.

I surprise him when I shift closer with a feral grin, positive his delight means he believes I'm actually giving in. Just for effect, I slip my hands around the back of his neck.

"You asked for this, you son of a bitch." I grit my teeth then slam my knee up into his groin as hard as I can.

His breath leaves him in a sudden rush and his eyes go wide. A pitiful, incoherent groan emerges from him as he shoves me back and doubles over.

"You bitch!" he wheezes, then lunges at me in a crouch. I take another step away, but my heel catches on uneven ground, and when I put my other foot back to regain my balance, I find nothing but air.

My stomach lurches as I lose my balance, arms flailing and a scream erupting from my throat. A second later, I plunge into the icy water of Dean Robertson's koi pond with nothing but the darkening, sunset-streaked sky above me.

CHAPTER TWENTY-SIX

GWEN

*T*he wave of panic that hits me has nothing to do with falling in the pond. I'm a fine swimmer, and it's also only a few feet deep, so I don't even get my hair wet. But my phone is in my pocket, and I hope to hell the water didn't damage it.

When I emerge, I'm only vaguely aware of the alarmed partygoers emerging from the house. Then several figures dart into view from beyond the bushes surrounding the pond.

"Jesus! Gwen, are you okay?" Lance yells, then splashes into the water himself, reaching me in a second. I grab his arm for balance as he guides me back toward the path at the side of the pond closest to the house. More people rush past, some heading toward Dr. MacArthur, who's curled into himself on the bench, muttering curses and crying assault.

"It was him," I say, still too dazed from the adrenaline rush to express a coherent thought.

"I know. We figured it out. Did he hurt you?"

I shake my head, looking back over my shoulder as Lance escorts me toward the house and a bench just outside the

French doors. "He tried, but I wouldn't let him. He pushed me…" Lance urges me to sit, then crouches in front of me. "My phone. Oh god, please tell me it isn't destroyed. I was recording him. I think I got him… He admitted to what he did to me." I scrabble at the sodden folds of my skirt, trying to find the pocket that holds my phone.

Dean Robertson emerges from the house then, his eyes going wide when he sees me. "Dr. Brennan. What happened?"

Before I can answer, Lance rises and sticks his nose in the dean's face. "I'll tell you what happened. That asshole MacArthur assaulted her—*again*. He was the one who attacked her last fall. You need to call the police and have him arrested."

"Phil?" Preston mutters, his mouth opening and closing in utter shock. "That's… That's not… You must be mistaken." He shakes his head and looks at me again.

I manage to fish my phone from my pocket and hold it up. "I recorded him this time. He admitted it. I have proof." At least I hope I do.

"Let me see," Preston says. Before he can take my phone, Lance grabs it.

"No you don't. We need to get this in a bag of rice fast. And if you know what's good for you, you'll call the goddamn cops and fix this, otherwise you can expect a lawsuit." He squeezes my shoulder. "I'll be right back, I promise. Don't go anywhere."

"Is this true?" says a firm, feminine voice. I look up to see the dean's wife, Vivian, standing in the open doorway Lance just disappeared through. She's a petite woman with gray-streaked black hair and flawless pale skin, who's always given the impression of being old-fashioned. She holds a large bath towel while staring accusingly at her husband.

The dean lifts a shoulder and spreads his hands. "It's true Gwen was attacked; you knew that already. But whether it was Phil... we can't be sure."

"I'm fucking *positive*," I snap.

Vivian scowls at her husband and reaches me, draping the towel around my shoulders, then sitting beside me and rubbing my back through the soft terrycloth. I tug the sides around me, grateful for its size and thickness.

"If she says it was him, you should believe her, Preston."

The girl I saw talking to MacArthur earlier edges toward us from inside the house. "I believe her," she says, her voice shaky. "I believe her because he did it to me too." She darts a look at me, her eyes dark with fear, but then she clenches her jaw and nods. "And I don't think I'm the only other one."

Dean Robertson heaves a sigh and lifts a hand to his face. "Christ, Phil," he mutters. He turns when a commotion reaches us from the bushes. A group of surprised people emerge, led by Percy, who has one hand firmly clamped at the back of Philip MacArthur's neck, pushing him forward while he holds one arm twisted behind his back.

The dean's eyes go cold and he sets his jaw. "Put him in my office. I'll call the authorities." He disappears inside, and Percy shoves MacArthur forward down the path toward the house.

"She's a lying whore!" MacArthur snaps.

Percy shoves him harder. "You need to keep your goddamn mouth shut. You're lucky I didn't wring your neck for what you did."

Lance reappears with a rice-filled kitchen baggie, my phone submerged within the grains. He glares daggers at MacArthur as Percy pushes past. Then Lance comes to sit on my other side.

"We've got him," he says. "Your phone doesn't look like it's too badly damaged and the recording saved, so this is just to be on the safe side. Ambrose and his partner are on their way over now."

"What's your name?" I ask the young woman still hovering nearby.

"Alexandra... Alex," she says.

"Do you know any of the other girls he might have assaulted?"

She swallows hard and nods. "I haven't talked to them, but I've heard things. I know who they are. I can message them now, if you think I should."

"Every bit of ammunition against him will help," I say. "We can't let him get away with this."

THE PARTY IS in chaos for the next hour. Lance's brother and his partner arrive with a detective, who insists that no one leave until he questions each guest about the events of the evening. Ambrose cuffs MacArthur and takes him away, and the other guests gradually disappear as they're allowed to leave.

The detective spends as much time with Alex as he spent with me, making a list of the students MacArthur allegedly assaulted. I get a peek at the list when he shows it to me to ask if I know any of the women. There are far too many names, and several are familiar—former students who've taken my classes, some of whom have since dropped out, and I can't discount the possibility that whatever he did to them had something to do with it.

Percy and Lance try their best to keep a polite distance, but are always in my periphery. I wish like hell they were sitting on either side of me, holding my hands. I don't need to start a scandal in the middle of all this, though, so it's better this way, but when the detective finally dismisses us, I'm so relieved I nearly collapse when I stand.

Lance is at my side in a blink, and Percy looks like he'd swoop in too, but holds back. Vivian watches us, her shrewd gaze flitting between the two men.

"I'll be fine," I say. "I just want to go home." To Vivian, I add, "Thank you for letting me use your shower and loaning me dry clothes. I'll return them to Dean Robertson next week."

She nods and comes close, giving me a tight hug and an air kiss against my cheek. Then she turns to Lance, her gaze darting between him and Percy, who's not far behind us. "Listen to what she needs. Make sure you take good care of her."

"That's the plan," Lance says. Percy nods silently.

Our ride awaits, a limo Chloe sent over after Percy messaged her with the news. When the three of us climb in, I'm past caring what the dean thinks, if he's even watching.

"Are we skipping the club?" Lance asks. "Because if we are, I'm going to ask this guy to slide into a drive-through. I'm famished."

Percy chuckles, but looks at me, eyebrows raised. "It's up to you. After tonight, I understand if you'd rather just unwind at home."

They're sitting across from me on the comfortable leather seats. I'm tempted to just defer to Lance's hunger when he fidgets and lets out a subtle hiss. I narrow my eyes, studying the way he's perched on the seat so much more carefully than Percy.

"You're wearing the plug, aren't you?" I ask.

His cheeks darken with a flush and he cuts a glance to

Percy. "I keep my promises. I wanted to be prepared if you were still in the mood."

"You know what? It's only nine. Let's go straight to the club. My outfit is there, and I could use a masquerade to wash away the memory of that bastard's hands on me."

Percy grins and slaps a hand on Lance's thigh. "Looks like we're on, kid. I hope you're ready."

CHAPTER TWENTY-SEVEN

LANCE

*M*y hunger pangs fade with the look Gwen gives me, and suddenly I don't give a fuck about food anymore. I want to devour *her*. But apparently I'm a little dense, because it takes a few seconds for it to sink in that *I'm* the one on the menu tonight.

I'd been sporting a half-chub ever since I lubed up the plug and shoved it in my ass during a bathroom break right before we left the dean's house. Percy's and Gwen's need is so palpable my dick gets fully hard, and I'd probably submit right here in the car if they suggested it.

But I'm forced to wait. At least the dean's neighborhood isn't far from Whitewood, so it's only about a fifteen-minute drive before we pull through the gates and around the circular drive of the house I snuck into more than a month ago. My stomach flutters when the door opens, and I step out, then reach in to help Gwen.

A silver-haired woman stands on the top step before the open doors of the huge Tudor mansion. Her blue gaze is laser-sharp when it scans the three of us. Sweat breaks out on the back of my neck, but she focuses on Gwen, opening her arms when Gwen climbs the steps to greet her.

"Percy gave me the news," she says. "I'm so glad your ordeal is coming to an end."

"Thank you for everything, Chloe. I don't know what I would've done without you. Without Whitewood, Percy... everything."

Chloe nods and leads Gwen through the double doors into a vestibule, where another set of doors open for them. I hesitate on the top step until Percy nudges me.

"You good?" he asks.

"Yeah," I say, then swallow dryly, positive I'm not very convincing.

"C'mon. She doesn't bite. Gwen and I both vouched for you."

"You sure I have to have this meeting? She looks like she just wants to talk to Gwen."

We're several paces behind the two women when we enter the house. I'm too distracted with the prospect of this interview I'm supposed to have with Chloe to really marvel at the decor. I just have the general sense that it's a fucking nice house. I'm also grateful there aren't too many people here—just a handful relaxing in a sitting room near the front. They afford us only passing glances.

Gwen and Chloe continue down a wide corridor, then pause at a turn. Gwen looks back and smiles at me and Percy. "I'm going to head up and get ready. I'll meet you two up there after Lance's interview. The masquerade doesn't officially begin until ten, so we have time"

Her smile softens when she sees me, and she steps close, placing a palm against my cheek. "You'll do great," she says, pressing a gentle kiss against my mouth. Then she turns and hits a button beside a door, and I realize there's an actual elevator when it opens to reveal the small interior. Gwen blows another kiss to me and Percy just before the doors close.

"Follow me, Mr. Lacosta. I have several questions to ask you, as well as some papers for you to sign." Chloe squeezes my forearm and turns, continuing down the hall to another door near the end.

"I hope I have the right answers," I say, wishing my nerves would settle down.

She leads me into a large office with a fireplace and gestures to one of a pair of chairs facing it. Between them is a bottle of wine, two glasses, a sheaf of paper, and a pen.

I stare at the seat, hoping the act of sitting doesn't wake my dick up again, because I really don't want to pop wood in front of this woman, sex club owner or not.

"Would you prefer if Percy waits in another room, or would you like him with you?"

"Uh, he's fine, I guess," I say, glancing back at him. "I mean, he knows all my secrets already."

Percy nods and moves to another corner of the room where there's a small sitting area with a sofa and coffee table. "I'll be here when you're ready."

I exhale and carefully sit. Chloe offers me wine, which I accept, grateful for a little alcohol to dull the edge of my anxiety.

"First, I don't bite," Chloe says. "Think of me as a mother hen. I consider everyone who enters those doors family, whether they're my employees or paying members of the club. Despite the fact you broke our rules on your first visit, I believe in giving you a chance to redeem yourself."

"I apologize for that," I say, "but I don't regret it."

"Thankfully neither do Percy or Gwen, which is why you're here now. Before we begin, I need you to sign this. It's a standard NDA, but it protects us both. What happens in Whitewood stays in Whitewood. Once you sign, I will explain how things work and what will be expected of you. You'll fill out this questionnaire about your preferences." She lifts the top sheet to reveal a several-page questionnaire. "Then, if you agree to the terms, you can sign this."

She flips the pages over, revealing something that looks like the first page of an employment contract.

"Of course," she continues, "you may have as much time as you need to read over it and consider the offer. Consider tonight's masquerade a gift."

"Sounds good," I say, stomach in knots. I scan the NDA to make sure there's nothing hinky about it, but it all looks above-board. I need to do my due diligence despite every cell in my body ready to dive in. I want this, so I doubt anything would keep me from saying yes.

But I already fucked up once, so I'm determined to follow *all* the rules to the letter to make sure I'm allowed to stay. I sign the NDA, then hang on every word of Chloe's lengthy lecture on Whitewood rules and expectations.

The questionnaire is a more extensive list of kinks and limits than those Gwen and Percy introduced me to during our first weekend together. After I complete it, she reviews my answers and follows up with a series of very personal questions. Thankfully she only scratches the surface of my childhood trauma.

By the time we finish, I'm relaxed and buzzed from the wine, my thoughts periodically shifting to Gwen and what she's up to. I accept the contract and stow it in my inside jacket pocket, promising to give it a thorough read soon.

When I stand, Percy is already at the door waiting for me, his face now covered in a bejeweled mask of deep green. He hands me my own mask, which is a black one similar to the one I stole that first night, only more ornate, with embroidered scrollwork amid the onyx gemstones.

I put it on as we emerge into the hallway. When the door closes behind us, I heave a breath. Percy starts back down the hall to the elevator, which arrives moments after he presses the button.

"That wasn't so bad, was it?" he asks when we step inside.

"No, but I still feel like I went through the wringer."

"It's worth every second. The contract is more than fair, by the way. I understand wanting to take your time to read it, though."

"Honestly, I'd probably sign anything to get to come here for the foreseeable future, but I'd be a failure of a wannabe lawyer if I didn't at least read the thing. I'd have done it in there, but I don't want to wait any longer to get into that room with you two."

"Understandable. Are you ready?"

"I've been ready all fucking day," I say, grinning at him when the elevator doors open on the second floor.

We exit to a familiar sight: a pretty girl wearing a striped satin corset and a bright smile behind the ribbon counter.

"Well, if it isn't Mr. I'm A. Giver returning to the scene of the crime," she says, looking at me. "I heard about you. Not too many people get away with breaking the rules here."

"I got lucky, I guess."

"Olivia, meet Lance, Whitewood's newest member."

"Are you wearing ribbons tonight, or are you part of the scenery? The others are still setting up," Olivia says.

"Tonight he belongs to Queen Justine, so no ribbon," Percy answers.

"Ah," Olivia says with a knowing smile. "Happy to have you as part of the family, Lance. Enjoy your masquerade!"

Percy leads me down the same hall I remember from my

first visit. Curtains are drawn across all the windows, and no guests are in sight, but there's one open door halfway down. When we pass, I peek inside and see Casey from my residence hall chatting with the two men she performed with last time I was here. I pick up my pace to avoid catching her eye, but she turns her head and lets out a surprised curse.

"What the fuck? Is that who I think it is?"

"Shit," I mutter under my breath. Percy chuckles.

"Lance? Lance-motherfucking-*Lacosta*?"

The next door down opens and Brit pokes her head out, followed by her boyfriend Adam and *their* Dom. The next thing I know, I'm surrounded by six near-strangers, and the only thing I can think of is that I have an enormous butt plug pressing against my prostate. It's all I can do not to get hard right now.

Brit's eyes are wide. "It was you who stole our masquerade invite last month, wasn't it?"

"Hey, I *found* the thing. One of you dropped it in the dorm lobby. I just happened to be resourceful enough to figure out what it was an invitation *to*."

Adam lets out a deep chuckle. "Nice work."

That's when I realize he's wearing full-on gimp gear, including shiny vinyl chaps covering both legs and black studded harnesses crisscrossing his torso. Both his nipples are pierced with hoops. My cheeks heat when my gaze drops to his groin, where his dick and balls are encased in some metal contraption with a fucking *lock* on it.

"Like the look?" he asks, spreading out his arms and twisting.

I cough into my fist and nod. "It's… ah… something. You are definitely not the all-American boy next door you look like at school."

"Looks can be deceiving," Brit says. "But in this case, Adam is exactly as kinky as that outfit suggests."

Thankfully she's in a robe, so I'm spared whatever costume she's wearing underneath.

"So you and Dr. Brennan, huh?" Casey asks. "You're a lucky guy."

Brit nods. "Be prepared for a crowd tonight, though. Femme Dommes are rare here, so she's popular. My suggestion is don't think about them. Keep your attention focused on the scene."

"Brit, you're forgetting he's already been here," Casey says. "I think if he was willing to dive in without knowing the rules, he'll be fine. Plus I saw the mods Rick made to Gwen's throne and the *extra* surprise they added. They've got something fun planned. We might need to just take a break and come watch too."

She grins at me and my skin goes a little clammy.

"We still need to get ready," Percy says and nudges me, his expression amused when I fall into step beside him again. After a moment, he asks, "Their presence isn't going to psych you out, is it?"

I take a breath, thinking about it, then shake my head. "No. I'm not really that self-conscious. I was more worried about watching them and getting inappropriately turned on."

"That's why they do what they do, though. The members come for a show, and when they're sufficiently worked up, there's usually an orgy in the ballroom downstairs, or any number of private rooms where members are allowed to play. I haven't been down to the ballroom since Chloe assigned me to watch Gwen, though. All I'll say is that the members get their money's worth… and here we are."

We reach a familiar door with the number 14 on the front in shiny bronze. He opens it and gestures for me to enter.

Gwen is seated on the throne, which has been joined by a second, nearly identical one. Both look a little different than I remember, outfitted with more handles, more hinges, and more upholstered cushions, though all the new pieces are neatly folded against the sides. The other change is the new, circular platform they both rest on close to the center of the room.

"You look… amazing," I breathe, not quite believing I'm here. She's wearing a sheer gown of ivory silk and gold threads that barely conceals her beautiful body. Her hair is coiled in a thick braid on top of her head, golden ribbons woven through it, topped with a gilt tiara. This is how she looked the last time, but tonight, everything feels different. Everything feels more *real.*

She smiles then, and the proprietary glint in her eyes is nothing like the Gwen I've spent the last month with. That's when I realize I'm no longer looking at Gwen; I'm looking at Queen Justine.

"And *you* need to get on your knees and kiss my feet."

CHAPTER TWENTY-EIGHT
LANCE

A melodic chime sounds over a hidden speaker system, and Percy rests a hand on my shoulder. "That means the masquerade has officially begun. It's time."

A motor whirs softly behind me, and I glance over my shoulder to see the curtains drawing open.

"Don't I get a warmup or something? You guys changed everything." I glance between them as I obey her order, stepping onto the dais and dropping to my knees before her.

"We adapted," Gwen says. "And Percy and I thought we'd rather surprise you than give it all away before our scene tonight—preserve some of the spontaneity. But you are more than welcome to safe word out of anything you don't like."

I grin at her. "The hell I'm backing out now. I am at your mercy, my queen."

Percy is at his post just behind and to one side of her throne. The other throne remains empty, and I can't help but wonder who's going to take that seat.

Percy's gaze heats as he watches me. "You must follow her orders. She commanded you to kiss her feet."

Goosebumps prickle my skin at the command, and my

dick twitches in my pants. Then Gwen slides her hand over the end of her armrest and toggles a small switch I missed until now. The platform we're on begins to rotate.

When the window comes into view, a throng of viewers are outside. I smile at them, then bend my head to do the queen's bidding.

Her ankles are both adorned with wide gold bracelets that stand out against her dark skin. I lower my lips to the top of one foot, kissing down the instep to her big toe. Then I switch to the other, gliding my lips in a soft caress.

"Higher," she says. "And you may use your hands."

"You honor me," I say, smiling up at her. I bend again, beginning above her ankle bracelets, kissing along the inside of her calf while I caress the other with my hand. The sheer fabric of her skirt parts up the center, either side falling away from her thighs. My attention flicks to her pussy poised over the open bottom of her throne. I'd love to be beneath it again, tongue buried deep, but I have a sense that tonight's fun is going in a very different direction than last time.

"You might not feel that way when you learn how I intend to use you, my sweet knight," she croons.

I work my way to her knees, which part to make room for me. "I am yours to use in any way you wish," I say, pausing to look at her.

"You are such an obedient servant. For that, I will grant you a single taste."

She lowers a hand to her pussy and spreads herself open. Her folds glisten with dewy wetness. I slide my hands up the outsides of her thighs as I lean in, determined to make the most of this.

My mouth is already watering, thanks to both my hunger and the prospect of having *something* to consume. I groan as my tongue meets her tangy flesh and sinks into her delicious wetness.

She sighs, resting her hand on top of my head and tilting her hips toward me the slightest bit. I know if we weren't expected to draw this scene out for a full hour, she'd allow me to keep going, but she pushes me away after only a few seconds.

"I realized something last month," she says, leaning forward to cup my cheek and drift a light caress over my cheekbone with her thumb. "Your mouth is too perfect not to share. So tonight, instead of *me* choosing a lucky supplicant to service me, I decided I'd allow you to choose one to service."

She hits the switch to disable the rotation of the dais, then rises to her feet, stepping to one side of the second throne while Percy moves forward on the other side.

I blink up at her, shocked at this development. I look from her to Percy, then back to her.

"Is this really what you want?" I ask.

"Only if you agree, honey," she says in a low voice. "You never have to do anything you don't want to do here—remember that. But tonight, in this scene, you are my plaything, and I wanted to try something similar to my usual masquerade routine. Part of the fun, the excitement, was always in playing with a stranger. You are a skilled performer; I think you know this. And there is power in making a choice to bestow your gifts on someone new. But if you would rather not, we will play just the three of us."

Her explanation makes sense, so I turn on my knees to face the crowd. Several women and a few men seem to lean closer to the window.

Adrenaline-fueled anticipation has my blood pumping. I don't have to pick anyone if I don't want to, but I admit I'm secretly turned on by the fact that Gwen has decided to share me with the club. She's a generous woman, and tonight I'm nothing more than her toy, an extension of her need to assert control over her own life. It might have bothered me, except that in the last month I've spent with her and Percy, not once has she tried to control me. She's been more kind and thoughtful and generous than I ever expected, to the point it's not an understatement when I say I would do anything for her. Percy and I were prepared to commit murder for her, but it was only her tender heart that kept us from following through.

It feels right to pay it forward tonight, but it can't be just anyone. I study the crowd, and in the second row, I see what I want—not just one person, but three: a woman and two men wearing light blue ribbons like I wore my first time here, and who look just as nervous as I felt. I'm willing to bet they're new to the club, though they're clearly here together.

All three are dressed up for the party. The woman's dark waves frame her masked face, and she's flanked on her right by a tall, broad-shouldered Black man and a more slender, blond white man on her left.

The man on her right bends down to whisper something in her ear. She shakes her head, then says something to the other man.

Both men are fit and attractive, as far as I can tell. They're probably close to my age, or maybe a little older. There's something familiar about the larger man, but with his mask on, it's hard to suss out. The woman is gorgeous, and she licks her lips when she meets my gaze. Maybe it takes being part of a threesome to recognize another threesome.

"Looks like he might have found someone," Percy says. "Tell me who and I'll bring them in."

"Am I allowed to pick more than one?" I ask.

"You may pick whomever you like," Gwen says. "Just remember they're for *you* to play with while Percy and I watch, if that's what you wish. But only one of them may take the second throne."

I glance over my shoulder at the pair of vacant thrones. So this is the plan. She's going to let another woman—or man—reign at her side for a night.

"And when is Percy going to take his turn with me?" I ask, lifting an eyebrow at him.

Percy smirks. "When the opportunity presents itself and you look ready, I'll check in with you. Now, who am I bringing in?"

"See the three near the middle—the younger woman and two men who look attached at her hip? I want *them*."

CHAPTER TWENTY-NINE

PERCY

I was on the fence about Gwen's decision to adjust our Masquerade scene to continue including guests. It was difficult to envision sharing her with anyone after spending the last month getting closer to Lance and falling into a comfortable—though highly erotic—routine with the two of them. I suppose it's because it's still very new and I don't like the idea of sharing them with anyone.

But when she explained her plan, I decided it couldn't hurt to try it once. Now that Lance has chosen another threesome—two men and a woman who look brand new to Whitewood—I begin to recognize the power we have here. Not to mention I can't wait to make use of the new adaptations made to the throne. It's configurable for all sorts of fun and interesting positions, not unlike the bench that Michael, Brit, and Adam use. And there are *two*.

I walk to the door and open it, then scan the audience, looking for the woman Lance pointed out.

"You in the blue mask with the feathers," I say. Her mouth drops open.

"Seriously? Um…" She darts an anxious look at her companions. "I'm not sure if they'll like it."

"They don't have to, because we want all three of you," I say.

"No shit. This place is better than I expected," her Black friend says. "Let's go, Kitty Kat. Sounds like we're about to get our money's worth."

The blond man's eyes widen and he glances at the window. "In front of everyone?"

His comrades are already halfway to the door when the woman named Kat turns back. "It'll be fun, Ben. Get your ass over here." She turns a bright, if a little manic, smile toward me. She's nervous, but excited, which makes it clear she's new to the entire scene. After initiating Gwen into the club's dynamics, I decided working with new members can be a lot of fun.

Ben falls into step and they enter the room. I direct them to stand in the center in front of the dais where Lance still kneels beside Gwen. She's gently stroking his head like he's a prized pet, and his dick is a prominent ridge in the front of his trousers.

I walk in front of the trio and face them. "I take it you three are new to Whitewood, is that correct?"

"Yes sir," the woman says.

I smirk. "No need to call me sir. I'm not a Dom. Queen Justine is in charge here, but it's my job to make sure you know the rules. First, do you consent to sex play with the members in this room? This may involve oral sex, as well as digital penetration. It may also involve fucking. Nothing happens unless everyone involved consents."

I frown and glance at Lance, then turn back. "You're here by invitation, correct? You didn't sneak in through the back or something?"

The woman's eyes widen and the two men laugh.

"Oh god no," she says. "Mistress Chloe is a friend of a friend, I guess you could say. We were invited."

"Good, then that means you've been properly vetted, which means you've also been thoroughly tested for STIs and can't get pregnant. No prophylactics are used during scenes. We value physical enjoyment above almost everything else, save consent. If there is anything you don't like, either use your safe words or simply say stop. What are the safe words you chose when you completed your interviews?"

I stop in front of the Black man and meet his eyes. Recognition hits when I'm up close, and I have to force myself not to react. It's Andre Kingston, who was the rising star of an East Coast NFL team until scandal hit—and I'm pretty sure I'm looking at the cause of said scandal standing beside him.

His eyes narrow and his jaw clenches as if he's ready to defend his decisions. But that's not what tonight's about.

"Safe word?" I prompt.

"Heisman," he says.

I nod and move to Kat.

"Anarchy," she says in a sexy drawl and gives me a flirty smile. She'll get the hang of things fast, but hopefully refrains from breaking the rules. Tonight's a big risk, but Gwen loves the idea of sharing the love one night a month, and I love making her happy.

I step over to their anxious third, Ben. He's relaxed a little more, having surrendered to his fate, I imagine, considering how much more dominant his partners are.

"Ginsburg," he says.

Behind me, Lance murmurs, "Nice." The kid is such a legal nerd. Hopefully he doesn't hit it off *too* well with these three.

"Good. Now for the rules of this room: What Queen

Justine says goes, so long as her commands don't violate your limits. That's it. Which of you will take the throne beside her tonight?"

Their gazes all shift to the dais behind me, and both men turn to the woman between them.

"Pretty sure this is you, Kitty Kat," Andre says.

"Excellent," I say, stepping to one side and gesturing to the throne with a slight bow.

Gwen strides forward then and holds out a hand to Kat. "Will you join me in my reign over these four subjects?"

"My pleasure," Kat croons.

"First, we must get you ready. You'll want to preserve that beautiful dress, but I have the perfect thing for you to wear. Come with me."

The pair walk hand in hand around the dais and disappear behind a door in the back. I turn to Kat's escorts.

"The four of us need to prepare for their return. Help me undress the queen's favorite subject."

I motion to Lance, who comes to stand in front of the other two. The men share a glance, which I watch intently for any indication they'll balk at the idea of touching another man, but neither one flinches.

Ben steps forward first, facing Lance. "I think I'm starting to like this," he says with a smile as he grips Lance's lapels. To me, he says, "Do we have to follow the instructions to the letter, or can we improvise? Am I allowed to touch... *kiss*... things like that?"

"If the subject doesn't object," I say.

Lance looks dazed, maybe even a little fevered, as if he's about to combust. "I want fucking everything," he says.

Ben's expression turns serious, his gaze heated. He leans in, and Lance meets him halfway. Their mouths lock, and the shiver that passes through Lance's body makes *my* dick hard.

Ben pushes Lance's jacket off his shoulders and Andre catches it, handing it to me with an amused smirk. Next comes the shirt, which Ben slowly unbuttons, his mouth moving over Lance's jaw and down his neck while Andre tugs his shirt off over his shoulders.

Ben drops to his knees and Lance is panting, his pent-up need palpable enough I can taste it. Goddamn, these two are perfect partners for a scene like this, both of them enthusiastic, but restrained enough to draw it out.

Andre presses his mouth to the side of Lance's throat and slides his hands under Lance's undershirt while he kisses and nips at his neck. His groin is pressed against Lance's ass, hips gently grinding, which has to be driving Lance crazy.

Ben's gaze rises as he unbuckles Lance's belt, then unfastens his trousers and pulls them down. He slides both hands up Lance's bare thighs, teasing his fingertips around the top of his waistband. Andre does the same from the back, his hand drifting over Lance's ass. He pauses at the very back, and Lance lets out a prolonged groan.

Andre chuckles. "You poor thing. No wonder you're so wound up." He drops to his knees and tugs the rear of Lance's boxer briefs down, revealing the flat black end of the silicone plug nestled between his cheeks.

"He's training," I supply. "For me."

Andre looks at me and nods, dropping his hand from Lance's ass. "Understood. Hands off the ass. Careful with him, Ben, he's a bomb waiting to go off."

Ben nods, his touch slowing as he carefully stretches Lance's waistband until it clears his erection. Then he pulls his shorts the rest of the way off.

Lance is breathing heavy, his cock stiff and thick and beautiful as it juts between his thighs. He just stands there as the pair rise again and move away from him.

"Something tells me you need to let him go first, whatever it is we do tonight," Andre says. "My balls ache just looking at him."

"It's up to the queen," I say. "Lance, you may kneel where you were again."

He heaves a shaky breath, then nods, carefully walking back to the dais and taking up his position between the thrones once more.

"Who's next?" Ben asks, looking between me and Andre. He's clearly getting into this now.

"I think you are," Andre growls. Ben grins when his partner moves in close and begins unfastening the buttons of his shirt. "You going to join me?" he asks, looking at me.

"It would be my pleasure," I say.

I hazard a look at Lance when I move behind Ben. He seems very self-contained, but the struggle in his eyes is evident and his fists remain clenched atop his thighs while he watches us.

Andre and I get Ben undressed. Then it's Andre's turn. Finally, the pair of them share the task of removing my clothes.

I'm wrapped up in the excitement, sharing kisses with each of them during the process, my skin electrified from the casual contact and barely there caresses. It's more polite than I would have expected from two horny men, which bodes well. They respect boundaries, which might come from sharing a very dominant woman. But they both still manage at least one *accidental* brush against my hard dick before I instruct them to line up in front of the dais on either side of me.

We're just in time for the women to return, and when Gwen and Kat appear, both of Kat's partners let out appreciative whistles.

Kat is in Gwen's other outfit, a gown of sheer blue silk shot through with silver threads. She's also arranged her hair atop her head similar to Gwen, with a small silver tiara nestled around the plaits.

They both give us delighted smiles when they step up on either side of where Lance kneels. He watches them, head twisting to follow as they move past him, linked hands passing over his head.

Gwen takes her seat again, smiling as she observes Kat, who pauses before the second throne, studying it.

"This is some kinky throne," Kat says. "I'm going to have *so* much fun."

CHAPTER THIRTY

GWEN

*T*he boys have outdone themselves tonight. I wasn't sure how my new idea for our little show would turn out, but it's going well so far. While I was helping Kat dress, she explained the situation with her men. They've been embroiled in a scandal in Washington, D.C., so they're scouting a new place to call home. New York is looking better and better, so there's a good chance if tonight goes well, they'll return and become regular members of Whitewood.

I like her, and feel even more comfortable with my scheme when I see Lance still kneeling, now naked, and the three other men lined up and ready to receive their orders from their queens.

"Queen Katherine, be my guest and choose a subject to service you to start the evening off."

"It would be my pleasure. Are they all an option?"

"Each and every one, if you wish."

She bites her lip, barely containing her excitement. "Gosh, it's so hard to choose, but I think I want Andre to get things going."

I nod at Percy, who directs Andre to the throne, then carefully arranges the backrest for him to lie on. Andre lets out a pleased chuckle when he pulls himself up beneath Kat's throne, and my own pussy tingles, because that first sensation is one of my favorite feelings.

Kat lets out a surprised gasp, then lets her head fall back, her back arched and her thighs spread while Andre services her with his tongue.

"Ben, get over here," she breathes, and her other partner eagerly joins them. The new additions to the throne allow him to straddle Andre's torso and face Kat, his knees resting on a pair of padded wings. She bends over and kisses him deeply, then leans back, sighing when he bends his head and kisses his way down her throat, tugging aside the fabric covering her breasts to suck on each nipple in turn.

Percy clears his throat, pulling my attention away from our guests. He tilts his head to Lance, reminding me something needs my attention before we do anything else. A promise must be kept.

Lance still faces away, his tattooed shoulders tense. The plug is visible between his cheeks, solidly entrenched inside him. It hasn't been that long since he inserted it, but I imagine it's been long enough.

"Lance, honey. Come to me."

He uncoils slowly, rising to his feet. When he faces me, he looks expectant and more than ready to be put out of his misery. I motion for him to approach my throne, and despite the passionate activity occurring beside us, his attention is wholly on me.

"You're fucking beautiful," he says.

I smile. "Are you ready?"

"For you, anything."

I nod at Percy, who rounds my throne and leans over to find the new lever just beneath the seat. The back reclines, then the arms fold down, becoming cushioned ledges just below the seat on either side. I lie back against the headrest and lift my feet to the ledges. I'm spread wide and on display.

Lance's gaze drifts over me, his breath quickening. "How many times would you like me to come tonight, my queen?"

I smile up at him. "As many times as you can stand, my love, but the first time will be inside me, with Percy inside you."

His eyelids flutter closed, a prelude to the relief he's hoping to experience soon. "Thank fuck," he mutters. He opens his eyes, his gaze more heated, less desperate when he coasts his hands down my inner thighs, spreading me wider. "I would love to eat you out right now, but I don't think I can wait another second to be inside you."

"Then don't."

He shifts closer, dropping to his knees on the knee-rest in front of the throne. My ass is perched at the very edge of the opening in the seat, giving him easy access to my pussy. He watches me intently as he aligns his tip with my swollen, wet folds. I'm more than ready, and let out a sharp gasp when he shoves in hard, then shifts forward to hover over me, hands braced on either side of my head while he starts to fuck.

"So fucking good," he murmurs, staring into my eyes, then looking down between us to where we're joined.

Percy moves back around us, and I'm absently aware of him taking care of little things. He hits the button on the throne again that triggers the dais to begin rotating, an addition we made to serve the audience a better view. He pauses at my side long enough to kiss me, then give each of my breasts a languid suck. On his way back around the throne, he rests a hand on Lance's shoulder, his other hand holding a bottle of lube. He coasts his palm down Lance's back and Lance quivers, his eyelids falling shut.

"Are you ready for me?" Percy asks.

"Yeah," Lance says, breathing heavy as his thrusts slow.

The activity beside us has slowed, and I can sense the other trio are more curious about us for the moment, but I'm too focused on Lance to care.

I reach up and curl my fingers at the back of his neck, urging him to kiss me as I raise my feet to wrap my legs around his waist. He lowers to rest on his elbows when our mouths meet, and his hips still. I hear the sound of Percy squeezing the lube, then feel the gentle brush of his hand over my leg when he presses it against Lance's back.

Lance pulls away from the kiss and looks at me, his lower lip trapped between his teeth. I can read the moment Percy enters him, because his hips twitch and his eyes clench shut, then spring wide, and he gasps.

"Jesus *fuck*!"

His mouth falls open and he begins to pant heavily.

"Hold still for a sec," Percy says.

All I can see is his hand curling over Lance's shoulder and gripping hard. Lance reaches back with one hand, and peering to the side, I watch him grip Percy's hip where it's pressed against his ass. Then he starts to move again, ferocious determination in his eyes. He fucks me harder and harder, and I have to reach up to grip the finials at the top of the throne to stay put.

"So fucking good," he says, eyes bright, cheeks flushed.

"Fuck yes," Percy says. "Squeeze me like that. Christ, I'm going to come so hard in your ass."

Lance's eyelids flutter closed, and he emits a long, low

groan, then opens his eyes halfway, staring at me in abject wonder. The way he looks at me sends warmth cascading through my body, and my heart flutters in recognition. I adore him. I adore them both, and after everything that happened today, I couldn't have imagined a better way to finish off our night.

Lance's face contorts a second later, and he throws his head back with a yell. His cock erupts inside me, his body coiled and tense as his hips jerk. Behind him, Percy's groan mirrors his.

I shiver with the pleasure of hearing them both come, the endorphins nearly as potent as if I'd climaxed myself, but I'm still a ways off from that. However, judging by the passionate sounds still filling the room, things have ramped up between the new threesome, and Kat's reaching her peak.

The men extract themselves from me and stand back, looking dazed, but happy as they watch the scene beside us unfold. Andre's face is buried in Kat's pussy and she's writhing on her seat. Ben has moved down to ride Andre's cock, his face contorted in pure bliss.

I'm entranced with watching them when a tongue swipes through my pussy, and I glance down to see both Lance and Percy leaning in between my thighs. Percy's tongue slides up through my cream-soaked folds, then Lance presses close, his cheek against Percy's and his tongue targeting my clit.

"Oh fuck," I groan as pleasure embraces me.

I close my eyes and surrender to their hungry, seeking mouths. The tongue against my clit flicks fast and light, then dips to push into my channel. The other glides lower to tease at my ass. I'm only dimly aware of soft conversation beside me, and a moment later, two mouths close over my nipples.

Ecstasy engulfs me then, overwhelming me with pure

sensory bliss. With two tongues between my legs and two mouths on my breasts, I lack the coherence to question Kat about her decision to share. I can only manage to turn my head, and when I open my eyes, I meet her gaze. She's sprawled on her throne, one leg hanging over the wide arm and her fingers working her pussy.

My orgasm begins to swell within me, but before it can take hold, Lance is above me again, his thick shaft filling me to the brim. He holds my legs wide as he pounds into me. Percy is at his side, teasing my clit and drawing the climax out of me with perfect precision. I arch my back, and the two tongues at my nipples keep up with as much frenzied abandon as I feel amid the pure, raw pleasure. My body tightens and the flood lets loose, drenching Lance's cock and balls and making everything ten times more slippery where we're joined.

"Fuck yes. Squirt your delicious cum all over me. God, I want to fucking *bathe* in you," Lance says, his words prolonging my rapture. He grunts and slams into me hard, coming again in tight spasms.

A breathy cry sounds, and I meet Kat's gaze again as she brings herself to orgasm, her triumphant smile saying everything about how tonight has gone for the both of us.

Through my blissed-out daze, I'm dimly aware of applause. I sit up and smile at the crowd as they pass with the rotation of our platform. Percy reconfigures my throne into its original position, and Kat and I both adjust our gowns, putting ourselves somewhat back together. She's flushed from the fun, and her men look like they're ready for round two.

"I think you guys need to take a bow," I say, halting the rotation of the platform when we face the window again. The four of them oblige, stepping to the front as if it's a stage and linking hands. They take a bow, and Kat and I both ogle their firm asses.

"I think this is going to be the start of a long and beautiful friendship," Kat says, then raises her hand up, palm facing me.

I high-five her with a laugh. "I agree."

CHAPTER THIRTY-ONE

LANCE

We all become *very* familiar with each other over the next couple hours, exhausting ourselves trying out all the new configurations the thrones can handle with six enthusiastic participants. By the end of our performance window, we've sufficiently broken the ice, but not a whole lot of conversation happens while we're playing.

Afterward, we clean up and spend the rest of the evening as guests watching the other exhibitions. I'm standing with the others outside another room on the second floor, watching a Dom play with a submissive who's bound inside a machine that looks like it came out of a science fiction novel, when someone taps me on the shoulder. I turn to see Olivia with a pleasant smile on her face.

"Mistress Chloe needs a moment with you," she murmurs. Gwen grabs Percy and we step away from the crowd.

"What does she need, Olivia?" Gwen asks.

"She didn't elaborate when she called up, just asked if I could send you down."

Stomach knotted with dread, I look at Gwen and Percy, but neither of them seem ready to offer any insight.

"We'll all go," Gwen says. "Whatever she needs to say to you, she can say to us too."

The three of us step into the elevator, but despite their comforting presence, my overactive imagination goes wild over all the possibilities. Did I break some rule I didn't know about? Should I have signed the contract before diving into the whole experience?

I know the other three are new to the club; maybe it's related to what we did with them. But the six of us established several unspoken rules on the fly, one of which was that no one should fuck someone outside their trio. Tongues and fingers were fair game, just no dicks going in holes below the waist.

That still left loads of fun to be had, and I learned more about sex tonight than I've learned my entire life before meeting Gwen and Percy. But the fact that everyone ended the scene more than happy with the outcome means I'm at a loss as to why the boss has summoned me.

We reach Chloe's door, and Percy leans in to knock. I hear low voices in conversation just beyond before Chloe calls out, "Come in."

But the other voice I hear is as familiar to me as my own, and the sound of it makes my stomach drop through the floor.

I grab the doorknob and twist, holding my breath as I push the door open.

Ambrose sits on the sofa in the comfortable seating area near the door and stands when we enter. He's in jeans and a button-down, so I know he's not here in an official capacity, but I still have no clue *why* he's here. He clears his throat, glances at Chloe, then back at me.

I pull off my mask, and we stare at each other for several heartbeats.

"Uh, someone please say something," Percy says.

Chloe and Gwen just look on with amusement.

I cough into my hand. "So, ah, what brings you here, brother?" I ask, feigning innocence.

Ambrose narrows his eyes. "In case you forgot, the three of you were part of a sexual assault investigation that came to a head earlier tonight. I've been calling you, Lance. You weren't picking up. I had no goddamn clue what happened. Maybe that asshole had friends he sent after the three of you."

My eyes widen. "You tracked my phone, didn't you?"

He nods and crosses his arm. "I'd ask you to explain, but Ms. Whitewood filled me in on everything I need to know."

"Tonight's only the second time I've been here," I say defensively.

To my surprise, my brother laughs. Then he sobers and swipes a hand over his face with a sigh.

"Listen, I'm just glad you're okay. I'm not here to ruin your fun. All I ever wanted was for you to be happy, and I'm over the fucking moon that you seem to have found your place. As long as school is still a priority for you, I won't stand in your way, okay? Now are we good?"

He stretches his arms out, and a lump forms in my throat. I close the distance and embrace him, enduring the tightness of his hug for as long as I can.

"You scared me, *hermano*," he murmurs against my ear. "Now that I know you're in a safe place, I think everything will be okay. But I still have *so* many questions."

I chuckle. "I'm not sure I'm prepared for this, but I'll answer what I can."

"We all will," Gwen says, reaching out a hand to my

brother. "We have an evening routine after a masquerade is done. Join us, and you can ask all the questions you like."

Chloe wasn't exaggerating when she referred to the club as her family. Evidently after every masquerade, all the permanent performers meet in a comfortable lounge on the first floor to share stories, drinks, and snacks. We meet up with our new friends and invite them to join us, and they enthusiastically accept.

Ambrose tags along, more subdued and curious than I've ever seen him, simply observing and listening for most of the conversation while I gorge myself on a sandwich Percy produces seemingly from nowhere. It turns out this place actually has a very well-stocked kitchen, which I raid before returning to the conversation fully sated and ready to focus on something besides my stomach.

The trio we played with drove all the way up from D.C. for the visit, and it sounds like they're planning to relocate permanently. It turns out Ben just graduated from Georgetown with a law degree, but hasn't taken the bar exam yet, since he was faced with the prospect of moving to a new state. We bond over our shared passion, and he offers himself up as a study partner when I start law school next semester.

Kat shares that she's currently interviewing for positions at economic think tanks in the city, with a few promising prospects. Andre remains quiet, seemingly happy to bask in the conversation and the plans his partners share. We've all figured out who he is, but so far no one has drawn attention to it, though Ambrose barely contains his fan worship. Andre is by far the most high-profile individual I've seen at the club, but I've heard other celebrities are members.

I notice Kat wears a pair of solid gold bands, one on each hand. I don't ask, but later the conversation comes around to how their trio got together, and we learn that she and Ben grew up as step-siblings. No one flinches, since such unconventional relationships seem to be a regular thing here; Michael was married to Brit's mother before she died, and Max was Casey's stepfather before her mother divorced him. Casey also shares a story about her best friend Sarah, who absconded with a pair of twins who used to work here, and they were apparently Sarah's foster brothers at one point.

"So yeah," Kat says, smiling down at her hands and the pair of rings she wears. "Ben was the one who proposed marriage. I married Andre publicly, but the three of us held a private ceremony and exchanged vows. We are all equal partners. It sounds like all of you have similar arrangements, am I right?"

"More or less," Michael says, giving Adam and Brit adoring looks where the pair are curled up on cushions on either side of his chair like loyal pets. But then I'm seated on the floor by Gwen's chair and Percy's stretched out across the rug with his head on my lap, so I definitely understand the dynamic now.

Kat gets up and slides onto Andre's lap on the loveseat he shares with Ben. "I think we found a home, baby," she says, kissing him, then pulling Ben's hand to her lips.

Ambrose has asked a few questions, but mostly he's just been taking everything in. He'll make a good detective one day when he gets promoted. I can see his gears turning with ideas about the club, and I can't wait to hear his thoughts next time I get him alone. He doesn't seem scandalized by it

—only curious. I think the fact that everyone in this room is clearly in a very happy, balanced relationship—however unconventional they may be—is keeping any reservations he might have about me at bay. In fact, he's looking at me with a kind of respect I haven't seen from him before.

I'm overcome with a strange emotion pulling at my chest and rest my hand on Percy's sternum. His eyelids flutter open and he stares up at me, then at Gwen, and places his hand over mine.

"Can someone loan me a pen?" I ask. Brit produces one from her purse and hands it to me. I retrieve the contract from my pocket, heart in my throat as I unfold it, speed-read the thing in two minutes, then lay it on Percy's chest to sign it.

"It's official," Percy says with a grin. "Welcome to the family!"

Everyone cheers. Someone produces a bottle of champagne a moment later, and Chloe joins us to join a toast to the four newest members of the club.

"It's a wonderful place to call home," Gwen says after the excitement subsides. She curls her legs beneath her and leans over my shoulder, combing her fingers through my hair as she pulls my head back to look into my eyes. "And always full of surprises."

She kisses me slowly, and my body goes languid under her touch. I feel drunk, despite the single glass of champagne. All I know is that I will do anything she asks of me for the rest of my life, if that's what she wants. And I hope it is.

IF YOU ENJOYED READING "The Queen's Knights" please return to the retailer to leave a review so other readers will know!

Get the erotic short epilogue to *The Queen's Knights* for FREE when you sign up for Ophelia's newsletter.

https://opheliabell.com/subscribe

Printed in Great Britain
by Amazon